# INFINITE KINDNESS

## Books by Laurie Blauner

### Fiction

*Infinite Kindness*
*Somebody, a novel*

### Poetry

*Other Lives*
*Self Portrait with an Unwilling Landscape*
*Children of Gravity*
*Facing the Facts*
*All This Could Be Yours*

# Infinite Kindness

## LAURIE BLAUNER

Black Heron Press
Post Office Box 95676
Seattle, Washington 98145
www.blackheronpress.com

Many thanks to Jenny O'Brien, Babs Lindsay, Gloria Upper, and Candace Dempsey, my good readers and appreciated friends, as well as to Gail Wilson, R.N., and Christine and Peter Kendell, my valued readers, who have shared their wisdom and time. Thanks also to Rich Ives and Michelle Sawtell, for their previous help. To my mother and sister for their support. And my husband, Dave Dintenfass, for everything. For the books that helped, including *Florence Nightingale and the Crimea 1854–55*, tso publishing; *Ever Yours, Florence Nightingale* edited by Martha Vicinus and Bea Nergaard; *Florence Nightingale: Letters from the Crimea* by Sue M. Goldie; *Florence Nightingale, Mystic, Visionary, Healer* by Barbara M. Dossey; and *Notes on Nursing* by Florence Nightingale. Publication of this book is made possible in part by support from 4Culture.

**CULTURE**
KING COUNTY LODGING TAX

This is first and foremost a work of fiction. All of the characters in this book are fictitious. Except for historical figures, any resemblance to actual persons, living or dead, is purely coincidental. Although I have tried to respect many of the historical facts, if they didn't suit my purposes I have changed them.

Black Heron Press
Post Office Box 95676
Seattle, Washington 98145
www.blackheronpress.com

For my mother

"The human species... generally ruin things in its own image, but it paid this price for its privileges: that the finite and specific animal body of this species contained a brain capable of conceiving the infinite and wishing to be infinite itself."

*The Corrections* by Jonathan Franzen

Part I

At the Thompson House, London, 1867

After I killed him he rose up in my dreams again and again. My first time. For the first one. But not after that.

His face loomed, cloudy, indistinct, Martin. I still remembered his wide nose, the terse lips in my dreams. He floated over a straw mattress. Nearby I held a knife high, bringing it down gently upon another boy's sternum, the surgeon's job. In my dreams the blood that was released arced in the air, a thin red waterfall that never seemed to end. I awoke to Martin's white body, enclosed in a uniform, the hovering face.

Once it had not been a dream.

His name was Martin Farland. The first thing he said to me was, "please, kill me." I nodded, ignoring him. Some men groaned in the background. My nurse's cap was tipped to the side; the day was already long. I probably sighed because he repeated himself, "Please, kill me." The first one. He was watching the boy next to him, blood pooling at his ribs, a dirty, red shirt, an amputation of the arm. The way Martin clutched his stomach, I thought: cholera or dysentery. That faraway look in his eyes. The terrible smell all around us, blood and sewers and everything else the body offered. A strip of light from the sealed, frosty window alighted upon his cheek, a bandage. I knew he did not have long, this body that haunted my dreams. I barely saw him, one face among so many. "I do not have anyone," his plea was frozen in the air between us. I nodded. Why not? Men I did not know were dying by the minute. My cap slipped off my head, disappeared among the straw mattresses, the barely visible floor, the dying men. I felt that fabric of sunlight upon my back, warming my spine. I took the photograph he offered me, slipping it into my pocket. "I do not have anybody else," he said. "Thank you." That was how I remembered it. My first one.

~

I awoke to the smell of breakfast. Late, I was late. Martin's face stared out my window as always. His nose plunged over his mustache, the thin, tight lips covered by the little wings of dark hair. His forehead was receding and surrounded with curly hair. The high-necked jacket of his uniform rose stiffly. My frame held him there, upon my night table. The photograph of him that survived the Crimean War. The face I have come, finally, to know well.

I immediately thought of Flo. The Florence Nightingale of legends. The woman who had brought me to Scutari, who carried a lamp at night, whose shadow soldiers kissed as it passed. How I had overheard her once in her barracks writing room, muttering as she wrote, her spine curved over her desk, "I am afraid this hospital shall become a bear-garden like Smyrna and Kullali with all the ladies coming here to get married and the nurses to get drunk. And the Irish nuns trying to convert the men on their death beds." A small bit of lace bonneted her dark hair and writhed about her neck, her tired, gray eyes were focused upon her paper. Who would soothe her? Then I had thought: she believes I am one of those ladies she is writing about. And I laughed, hard and loud.

I placed Martin face down, turned my own daguerreotype toward me so I could see my eyes, what I needed to resemble in a hurry. I combed, parted, and tucked my hair at the back of my neck. Then came the layers of clothes. First the cotton stockings, the drawers, a chemise, a corset. Next the petticoats, matching bodice, skirt, the numerous buttons, unending ties and hooks, lace flapping at the edges like an upset bird. I had given up maids since the Crimean War and said I had wanted to dress on my own as I had learned to do there. I discovered how to omit layers and my mother and sister were disgusted. But that day I was sorry. I flew down the stairs and rushed to the breakfast table.

"Ann, you are decidedly too late for breakfast," James said, pushing his heavy chair back and standing up. *The Daily News* was folded across his half eaten eggs, his nearly full teacup. They had not finished eating.

"Too late this morning for many things," Mrs. Thompson, my charge, said, brushing crumbs from her blouse, her eyes tearing.

It was then that I noticed Mr. Thompson's reddened face, his eyes were still open, fallen into his eggs. His tea was stain-ing the white tablecloth into an ocean pattern, a map with land and sea. Again that morning I thought of the Black Sea, Turkey, the Bosphorus. I returned his cup to his saucer in an upright position and suppressed my desire to finish the map with the remaining liquid. His copy of *The Times* lay upon the floor, his arms dangled from the table. His mouth was slightly open as if trying to take in air or food. His body slumped into his fa-vorite, needlepoint chair. I lifted one arm over the table by the wrist and his fingers swung back and forth over the sugar bowl.

Mary flattened herself against the wall and covered her mouth with her hand. Her other hand was still holding a teapot.

"I am so sorry," I said to Mrs. Thompson, a friend of my family.

"Perhaps he should have taken the water cure at Malvern last month instead of me."

"Mother," James turned toward her, "I shall help you upstairs and then Ann shall attend to you." He did not look at me.

I watched her handkerchief flutter by the doorway and she went slowly up the stairs. I heard him tell her at the banister, "This is the type of situation that she is well suited for."

"It was so awful, so fast. Mary was pouring us tea over breakfast one minute. And the next my dear husband was gone." Her voice fading.

I sat in my chair and saw my reflection in the empty plate, the hasty, dark hair, and large, dark eyes. The way my face was thinned to nothing upon the side of my untouched, white teacup. I was to clean up. Again. I thought of Hera, an owlet given to me by Florence who loved her own owl, Athena, so much that she believed she saw its ghost winging toward the fleshy, white moon on the day of the Sebastopol Report. "A tissue of lies." I imagined Hera soaring over the graves of soldiers on my last day there. All the way home, to an England that had been forever changed.

I ran my finger round and round the golden rim of my cup. My finger wiggled into the handle resembling an animal hiding from a predator and I lifted the cup toward Mary, as we were the only two living people left in the room. She hugged the walls of the room with a scraping sound, her back sliding against the wallpaper with its depiction of roses in splatters of

red and green. There was the utmost space between her and
Mr. Thompson as if he would leap up toward her. She sidled up
to me and began to pour.

   But I stopped her after the first splash. Her face was shattered bone porcelain. Her skirt was nervous against the legs
of my chair. I heard the slight chatter of her teeth. Perspiration webbed her forehead and neck. I peered at the top of Mr.
Thompson's balding head at the end of the table. "Two gills
of wine instead, please, Mary." Her eyes were startled but she
went to the cabinet and lifted the bottle. I knew that I would
receive whatever I requested.

   I wanted to tell her not to be frightened. "There is nothing final in the universe of mind or of matter—all is tendency,
growth." I was not certain I believed it, but it seemed comforting. For even science was tendency, growth. I wanted to kiss
her cheek, advise her not to cry. A strand of hair loosened from
the back of my head and brushed gently against my jaw. For
she was more frightened by the fact of Mr. Thompson's death
as compared to his strange rages from drink when he was alive,
especially with him bothering her as she had whispered to me
once, needing to push his hands away from her hips. The sun
outside swam among the clouds, moved tiredly into the room
and rested at Mr. Thompson's sodden feet. Patches of blue sky
the colour of veins beneath skin peeked at us. I wanted to explain to her how death had given me a whole new life.

                                ~

   After I had finished my glass of wine, after I had watched
daylight, which sat in an armchair and then moved to the rug,
ambling across the furniture, Mary and the cook disappeared

from sight. I thought about God. How He had visited Flo three
times so far and had not yet given me the time of day. I thought
of Mr. Thompson with his nodding, shiny head and complain-
ing voice meeting Him. It would not go well. What would they
talk about? Perhaps the good weather we had been enjoying
lately. "It is I. Be not afraid." That was what He told Flo the
first time she had seen Him and she had it framed upon a wall
at her house on South Street. Or so I had heard, as I had not
seen her in years, since the end of the war in 1856, eleven years
ago. I had not attempted to see her as yet because of the small
discomforts that had passed between us. But I had written to
her. I went slowly up the stairs, feeling the curve of the ancient, wooden banister. But James was still there, just leaving
his mother's room, his coat already on and I did not want to
see James.

"Business," he said to the doorway, "important business
and new discoveries."

"What could be more important than your father?" A voice
from inside the room.

But I knew that her words were wasted. His father was
gone. There were so many little wars that stayed with us that
were as yet unresolved. "The doctor has been sent for, Mother."

He glared at me. I heard, "But no one has even cleaned the
egg off his face yet," as he closed the door.

"She could jolly well do it. Or do something around here
for a change," he whispered to no one, really.

I looked at the sudden gust of his blonde hair, his blue eyes
fixed upon the door downstairs. I could hear horses passing in
the street outside, feel the shadows of vans and carriages going
by, so much life outside. He grabbed my arm a little too hard.

I stared at him and my other arm squirreled by my side. He pinched me at the elbow. "Your breath stinks. A regular nurse you are now."

I did not say anything but I turned my head away. A servant crossed the hallway downstairs with yellow primroses in her hands. I gasped and then he was satisfied and went down the stairs, hurried out the door. I hesitated outside Mrs. Thompson's bedchamber.

"Ann dear, is that you?"

But I did not say anything.I tiptoed to my bedchamber, down the hall. When I closed the door behind me I sighed. It was hard enough in my own family's house and I had hoped it would be better at the Thompson house, nursing Mrs. Thompson, although I did not know them terribly well. I had met James as a young girl, calling him "Slim Jim" when they would arrive at our house occasionally for tea. He was a sullen, older, quiet child with his rug of blonde hair. He watched me nurse my sick dolls, calling me "Pain." "Little Pain," he would say politely, "would you like another biscuit?" My mother was pleased at the recent invitation to take care of Mrs. Thompson again. She believed James would help me forget Martin Farland and the war. Little did she realize that her aim with James would succeed and that, with my rejection, he would come to hate me. Without really knowing me. But then who did truly know me? I thought of my own room at my family house with its bookcase full of science books, Notes on Nursing, government Blue Books, papers from the Royal and Sanitary Commissions. Tennyson and Longfellow. Books full of clippings like overstuffed chairs. I enjoyed the way flowers from the garden outside my room peered at the mystery of me, knocking their colourful, lush heads against my window. The trees that rose up behind them, branches bending and sometimes snapping in a good rain. If I closed my eyes I could imagine footsteps there, in a sort of marching. It was good enough that I had learned what I liked to do.

This room with its pale frills upon the bedcovers and window sashes, the pink fringes hanging from a runner along a dressing table, had belonged to their daughter Rose, who had died at nine of a fever. I had removed her dolls from the plump single bed and pink silk chair and placed them at the side of a bureau. They disappeared the following day. I had folded her child-sized coverlet at the foot of the bed and a sensible blanket replaced it the next day. She had never changed, grown up. When I opened her window I could not touch any newly emerging flowers, being above the ground floor. There was only air. I could place my hand through the nothingness, reaching toward the distant gardens and trees. I knew that being a memory had a large place in this household, as with many other households.

I took out a sheet of writing paper and began:

*My Dearest Flo,*

*I am unhappy here, as I am unhappy everywhere it seems. I am simply exchanging one difficult family for another. Each with their own eccentricities and sorrows and, sometimes, even joy. I do still miss my departed father, who educated me and my sister, as your own father did you. But my mother and sister shall not miss me, having enough parties and social engagements to keep them busy while I am gone. They call my work "a shameful attachment" which they believe they shall soon rid me of. Even after the Crimean War, even after all you have done to show that nurses are no longer all drunks, servants, or prostitutes. I showed them the article about Dr. Elizabeth Blackwell and her achievements in* The Times *and all they said was, "Well, that is the United States. And she is still unmarried." They laughed with each other.*

*As you have said of your own mother—they do not think of their children. When a pretty, young girl marries a rich man the children come unbid. And daughters are the property of their parents, then the property of their husbands. It is tiresome. Especially when I, like you, want to do God's work and it is a constant struggle to be able to do so.*

*My sister came into my room when I returned from Scutari and took all my dresses and jewelry, saying, "You do not need these anymore. You have often said that they do not mean anything to you." At sunrise my dresses were found cut into pieces and strewn among the wilting flowers of the garden. A quilt and my jewelry were discovered buried beneath mounds of overturned earth at the roots of cedar trees. The same sister who had lain across the threshold of our front door when I was leaving for the war and said, "Think of the family."*

*Well, I have thought of them, more often than they have thought of me. Because I have to. They are the windows and doors I look out of, planning my escape. And I shall be free one day, as I know you have struggled to be also.*

*I am sorry to burden you with my difficulties but I know that you alone can understand. I still miss Scutari where we were so needed and busy with God's healing work, "our 18,000 children," where every detail was important. And we could simply be ourselves. I have not done enough nursing since then except for the care of ill relatives or friends of the family.*

*I have heard that you are thinking of moving permanently to a hospital to live. I am sorry that you are in such constant pain and are unable to see visitors or go out. Perhaps the injections of opium will help you. Clarkey confided to me that she was turned away from your door and was unable to see you. I shall hope to make an appointment to see you soon.*

*Yours very truly,*
*Ann Russell*

I went downstairs and slipped the letter into Mary's still shaking hands and told her to deliver it to Thomas, the little orphan drummer boy that Flo brought back as one of her "Crimean treasures." Mary raised her eyes to mine slowly so that I could see her eyelashes touch her eyebrows.

"He ain't been picked up yet, Miss. He's still lyin there, his mouth full a eggs."

"He is garnering more buz-fuz now than when he was alive," I said as I hurried through the drawing room, the hallway, and into the dining room. The portrait paintings and velvet curtains became a brown blur. I thought of the Great Stink in London in 1855—I was in the Crimea then but I heard that the River Thames had so much sewage in it people vomited in the streets. As I cleaned off one side of Mr. Thompson's cheek with his unused napkin the eggs tumbled down onto the tablecloth like moss falling off of an old, dead tree. I thought of Martin again that morning as I always did with a death. Martin's face gone slack. I held Mr. Thompson by the back of his collar and then pulled him back into his chair. He slumped to one side. He looked to be clean enough except for a bit of egg still inside his open mouth. I felt my Hera swoop by me with her small, triangular wings, her melancholy cry, and I missed having her upon my shoulder, accompanying me wherever I went, a witness to my life. I still saw Martin's quieted, released

countenance or that of a soldier struggling and contorted in
pain when a man died so I stopped looking at their faces, concentrating instead upon their bodies, their unmoving limbs. I
could not avoid Mr. Thompson's plump, red, and vein-marbled
face this time. If Mr. Thompson had been a poor man they
could have used his body for science.

I sat at the window in the drawing room to better view
the anemones and snowdrops sprouting there. When I looked
upon the garden and trees, even when done blooming for the
year, all drooping and brown, I was in the present moment, not
the past with its wars or the future with its promise of work.
Not the barracks in Scutari, or with Hera, or Flo or my family,
nor the sick children I hoped I could help. I felt clouds moving
within me, and the sky's tranquility even as birds, sudden as
ghosts, scribbled their birdly messages against its lovely blue.
I was in the room, with brown curtains, a soft, pliant chair,
and a spray of flowers in a vase that mimicked the ones just
outside. Mr. Thompson tilted toward the floor in one room and
Mrs. Thompson waited upstairs, in the bed of another room.
The footsteps behind me were Mary's. She held out a drinking-glass of wine, misunderstanding my momentary rest. I had
only been visiting the Thompsons for several days, for the sake
of Mrs. Thompson's health. It was those alive I was more afraid
of than the dead.

I shook my head, "No, thank you, Mary." She did not move
for a few minutes behind me. She did not make a sound, as if
she was seeing what I saw, with me there and then. I turned as
she was leaving, almost out the door, and I saw that the wine-
glass in her hand had been emptied.

I went to the hallway, stepped outside without a shawl. Air
reeled around people on their way toward Hyde Park, women

in endless dresses that swept the pavements, wheeling infants whose heads pulsed from their prams. I held a section of railing as a horse's mane brushed my hand and my own hair raised along my arms as if at attention. The horse swiftly disappeared down the crowded street pulling its plain carriage. Clouds were gathering like women's white hats tipped together as they gossiped. The spiky rose bush across the street was beginning to bud behind its iron fence. Dabs of red winked at me between the sweep of people and carriages. My family house near Nottingham was far too quiet. I could not tell the clouds from smoke. It seemed that there were many more people in London than last year when my family and I visited briefly, even after the cholera epidemics. At the Broad Street Pump a few years ago Dr. Snow told the government, "Remove the pump handle" and that had stopped the epidemic. The answer had been so simple and so scientific. A clatter of heels and hooves and wheels and voices filled me. The air grew dirty and noisy around me.

A man walked past as large as a tree, a blossom of rain was at his shoulders. He was talking to a young woman who spoke to his chest.

"It is because of the Poor Law that the workhouses are so full," she said, her stylish bonnet rustling.

He touched his hat for droplets. "It is because of Parliament and the Tories." And then they were gone.

I stepped back toward the door; the windows of all the houses in neat rows across the street were staring at me. People were too busy to notice. A sudden wind drifted about my ankles. I was tempted to pet it—or to catch it by its tail. Too much life. I went inside, shutting the door behind me and the crowds became a whisper. I wiped some dust from my nose. I could hear Mrs. Thompson crowing at Mary.

"Ask, ask. I have to beg for every little thing here. You cannot even remember my tea."

Mary rushed down the stairs, a fast, wispy cloud. The scullery door closed forcefully. In my room I took out my medicine chest. The glass bottles clicked upon the top shelf as I examined the carbonate of magnesia, quinine, carbonate of potassium, ipecacuanha wine, and paregoric elixir. I searched the two drawers underneath past tonic pills and powdered rhubarb and finally found the James' Powder. I retrieved sixteen grains from the tin and poured some port wine into a drinking-glass.

Mrs. Thompson was in her bed when I entered her bedchamber, a night bonnet fringing her forehead, her arms resembled cold, white fish pocketed along the edges of the bed. A shawl tethered her shoulders to a pillow. She was pale and agitated, more so than usual.

She swallowed the powder and wine I gave her immediately. "Named after your son," I smiled. I sat by her bedside.

"You are a comfort to me, Ann. James has gone out on business at a time like this." She turned the empty drinking-glass in her hand over and over until a shaft of light appeared at my hem and then abruptly left, soon tumbling back again. "He is with his friends. He now owns everything."

She did not need to tell me. I thought of my own inheritance. My father had left me a small sum of money, apart from what was left to my mother, afraid I would never marry. "I should be leaving soon Mrs. Thompson. Going home."

"I could not help noticing the photograph of the handsome, young man at your table."

"I am sorry that I moved Rose's belongings."

"I should have had them removed long before you came. But concerning that handsome soldier."

"He was my fiancé, Martin Farland. He died in the barracks hospital in Scutari during the war, along with many other men I tended to."

"I am so sorry, my dearest Ann. I trust that you are comfortable here."

"Yes, thank you, Mrs. Thompson."

"I hope you will be able to stay a little while longer. My strength has improved but little lately. And with the death of my husband..."

"Yes, of course." I thought of being allowed to see Flo again instead of writing her letters. Of being allowed into her drawing room, to touch her cheek and heal her. She had once told me that her mother had written to her, "You would have done nothing in life, if you had not resisted me."

"Now tell me about the war. How brave of you to go." Her handkerchief fluttered about her face, dabbing at invisible perspiration.

I could not tell her that I would have gone mad for want of something to do, that my prospects for marriage were dull as often-trod carpets, that the world had pushed me into a corner. I had gone for a greater need and found a higher calling. "Many men died. We were all strained to the utmost in body and mind." Most people did not want to hear about the amputations and removal of bullets, the lack of hair mattresses and food and clean shirts, about the cholera and the other diseases that ran rampant.

"I hear you knew Florence Nightingale well. The famous lady with a lamp."

"Yes, I did but I have not seen her as lately. She is ill from

the war and a very kind and knowledgeable person." I adjusted her pillows, tidied her table. "I will open this window more
for you and order you some beef tea and custard."

"And I will write to your mother and ask her to allow you
to stay longer now with the shock of Mr. Thompson's death. I
will explain the situation to her."

"Thank you, Mrs. Thompson." I walked to the door.

"London is lovely this time of the year. Please tell Mary to
bring my little Chinese dog up here. The little beast kisses my
chin and throat. And the invitations to that pauper's charity
ball and the St. Thomas's Bazaar. Perhaps, with your help, I will
soon be well enough to go."

I found Mary wiping the grease of cold meat and pigeon
from the parlour mantelshelf and the wooden arm of a chair
where she said Mrs. Thompson would creep and eat at in the
middle of the night. Mary rolled her eyes when I mentioned
the dog. She was employing a rag to rub the head of an angel
who sprang from the leg of the chair. I sat at the piano near
the dark green velvet curtains and hoped that my own music would overtake me and lift me away. I would have liked a
household of my own, one of my very own making, without
the need of family or a husband. One like Flo's, but without her
Crimean illness.

I played Handel and Bach, my smooth hands crossing over
each other. Between notes I heard rain knocking at the outside
of the house. Through a slit in the drapes I saw water pooling
about the grounds of the garden, and in the unopened buds
of trees. Branches staggered underneath its weight and force. I
heard a dog bark somewhere, a wet bark. I played that gossipy
music even as rain worried all that was outside, forming clear,
round jewels upon all that had a surface. I was concentrating

on what was inside, that which I needed to tend to. I thought of Martin's face floating above my night table and how terribly convenient he was. The liquid wheeze of birds taking off from a tree just outside filled the room.

There was a knock at the front door and Mary hurried, avoiding the dining room altogether. I realized that it was silent in the room since the birds left, that I had not played a piece for a few minutes. I heard the stamping of feet and an umbrella shaken and closed. The front door was shut against the wind and stammering rain. Footsteps went upstairs and I heard murmuring voices. Then the footsteps came downstairs, circled about the dining room, and approached the threshold of my room. My piano was between us as two figures appeared at the door.

"This here's Doctor Carroll," Mary said and disappeared from view.

A middle-aged man with spectacles and a frock coat entered the room. His whitening hair tufted over his collar and tie. "I wanted to meet the woman who has been taking care of Mrs. Thompson."

"That is me, Dr. Carroll." I stood.

"I noticed adequate ventilation and light. And have you used a cleaning solution?"

"Yes, Sir William Burnett's solution of chloride of Lime."

"So, you were in the Crimean War?"

"Yes, Dr. Carroll."

"And do you adhere to the miasma theory or the contagion theory, Miss Russell?" He rubbed his muttonchops.

"I believe infection poisons the air. Patients breathe that terrible air and become quite ill. As in the barracks hospital, when it was over-crowded and poorly ventilated the fever spread among the sick and the staff."

"Hmm. Miasma. Not through direct or indirect contact between people? You do not believe in these 'invisible seeds' or 'clouds of tiny insects' passing between two people?"

"No, Dr. Carroll." My hand was cool resting upon the smooth piano. I offered, "I believe it was Mr. Thompson's heart that gave away, from the circumstances."

Dr. Carroll nodded. "I will take care of Mr. Thompson's body." He pulled his spectacles from his nose. "Do you have your own set of instruments?" He wiped his lens with a handkerchief and returned the spectacles to his face.

"Yes, with all manner of locking forceps and hemostats and clamps."

"Good. Very good. Are you too busy here with Mrs. Thompson?"

"No, Dr. Carroll. She is an easy case."

"Would you like to help at St. Thomas's hospital? The hospital is in much need of help and I shall obtain Mrs. Thompson's permission."

"Yes." I surprised myself. "Why, yes."

"Mary," Mrs. Thompson called from upstairs but Mary was nowhere to be seen. "Ann, are you there?"

"Perhaps Mrs. Thompson has a touch of influenza," Dr. Carroll smiled slightly as he adjusted his spectacles across his nose. "Perhaps she will need leeches."

"Yes, I think she will." I looked down to hide my smile, wondering whether he was punishing her with the leeches or not.

"I will see you tomorrow then."

I ran my hands randomly over the piano keys, hands that were able to do so much more. The sound was a leap in notes—

changes as in marriage, death, birth. I looked forward to my
new work, at a hospital again. The noisy rain imitated someone
talking, who was not pausing for breath. Who was not listening to what was being said. I closed my eyes. My mother and
sister loomed. Even Mrs. Thompson and James. Only my father
listened to me and so had several soldiers, when I tried to save
their lives.

For, like the piano, I was to be someone's property, always.
Either family's or a husband's who would have a spinster. A
stranger's. Perhaps God's one day. For I was close to thirty-two
years of age. I was immersed in the lives of these other people
without meaning to be. Alone, at night, I read—after all else
were asleep in the house. Travel books. About Egypt and the
Nile—with its slave markets, deserts, cautious crocodiles. I
imagined being clothed in sand, an efreet, a demon, digging
me out. There was too much sky there trying to flatten all the
bodies into the shifting hills. A footstep in any direction was
erased. Some of the girls and boys sold into slavery who escaped often could not be found again because there were no
traces left of them. There were the tombs and the pyramids,
beaten by the sandstorms for just existing. The remains of a
great civilization ran through our fingers. Hieroglyphics like
dreams rearranged by wind. Beyond them existed a devouring
silence. Rocks described themselves against a brow of sand.
The self was missing and then gone during travel. I did not
think of myself but only the different lives of others. Such was
how I thought of Egypt—although it was still someone else's
words and life.

I felt an insect crawling along my hem with the horsehair
braid but it was too much trouble to scratch it away. Luckily it
fell when I stood. I removed my boots and tiptoed up the stairs

where I removed the paper and pen again.

*My Dearest,*

*I will see "our children" again, in a manner. Patients—not soldiers—soldiers of disease. The suffering and helpless—those whose existence is somewhere between this life and the next. I have, so far, been taking care of ladies—some are relations—in their homes. But they do not know struggle or strife or Truth, half the time. They do not want to know it. The English drawing room is enough. But now I shall be pressed into service again by a Dr. Carroll at St. Thomas's hospital. It has been a while since I have done more than recommend Cod Liver Oil or arrowroot or helped with the tubes and leeches before they are laid upon a willing vein.*

*Mrs. Thompson is preoccupied with nothing so far as I can see except social appointments and now, the death of her husband. James shows his disappointment in me by trying to hurt me in little ways. They will bury Mr. Thompson soon and I must say that I will not miss him with his fearful obscenities or his breath that stank of drink. But it is still better than my own household that thinks so little of me.*

*I often think of love but understand that I must find it elsewhere—a metal buttonhook, red tulips, a church door, even in the lice on the head of an innocent child. The body lives on and seeks what it needs. I am so used to eating bread that I reject sugar-plums when offered—having remembered that they did not taste nearly as good as they looked.*

*We must be true to ourselves—even if the selves we show to other people are false. I have left Martin's photograph facing the table all day today. He was merely a lost child. He does not care what I do to him now. But he is a help to me.*

*I wait to hear the voice of God, letting His will be known. Although I know my calling without Him. As you have said, my occupation will make me One with Him.*

*Writing to you is like writing to myself, reminding me.*

*Yours truly*

# The Hospital

It was visiting day at St. Thomas's Hospital, which was housed at Surrey Gardens until the larger hospital with a pavilion floor plan designed by Flo could be built. Surrey Gardens was like a woman who did not reveal herself at first glance. She had nooks and crannies and spaces hidden away. While the new hospital would be one open room after another, large and square. No secrets, no places to hide.

In the front of St. Thomas's hospital was a fountain of piled up angels spouting water among the budding trees and early flowers, facing the eyebrow-shaped windows of the hospital itself. It was there, on my way inside, that a woman fainted clear away. I saw her bonnet one minute and next I saw her boots. Two men restored her, doctors by the sound of them.

"I do not feel a fever, Henry." One, with a bony face, said placing his palm on the woman's forehead. I glimpsed her smooth, pale skin, and pleasant, unconscious features, the tufts of her blonde hair.

"Could be headaches. They are going around," the one with the beard replied.

The woman, newly revived, was standing, leaning her hand on the scalloped ridges of the fountain. Her golden hair flew from beneath her bonnet. "You can take your hands off of me, Sir. I am perfectly well. I am here to see Mrs. Drake. Do you know which room she is in?"

"I do. She is in my ward," the bearded one said. "Follow me."

When I nervously entered the wards children were scampering about. A few knocked over a plant and tilted a picture of a once serene landscape that now had some scrapes about the hills and sky. Some of the beds had visitors sprawled across them, with some people overflowing on the sides. While other patients had no visitors and lay back upon their pillows with their eyes closed to the wan sunlight. A fistful of new flowers lay strewn across the legs of an older man who was tossing about his bed. The smell of pus and blood and perspiration lay underneath the scent of flowers and chloride of zinc. A few nurses were attending patients but there were not many of them, obviously not enough. I noticed their lavender eau de cologne. I had forgotten mine. It had been quite a few years since I had worked in a hospital. A man with his cloth curtain half hiding his bed was waving the stump of his bandaged arm in the air, yelling. I relaxed and felt at home. I was needed.

My ward had a mix of about thirty patients. The doctor with the beard was the head of my ward, Dr. Henry Lawrence, and the woman who had fainted was at the bedside of a slightly older woman with thrashing dark hair and eyes that appeared to be enlarged because of her pupils. Puerperal fever. I wondered where her child had disappeared to. I touched the visiting woman's shoulder.

"Are you feeling better?"

"Yes, thank you." She whispered to me, "It must have been these insufferable undergarments. However, I am more worried about my friend here." She pressed a wet rag to her friend's forehead.

"How is the patient?" Dr. Lawrence bellowed, pushing the curtain aside.

"Her fever is increasing."

He bent down and examined her, her skin was damp and her black eyes rolled to the top of her head when he pried the lids open. "Yes, yes, I can see that. I have just come from the dead-house where another woman had the same fever. Miss Russell will fetch some sago and preserved meat from the kitchen."

I went down the well-used wooden stairs, through the cellar, to the kitchen for the order and on my way back up I saw a rat chewing on a bit of something that snapped at the close of its teeth. The strong smells of food from the kitchen wafted by. A woman in a tattered dress with a chemise showing clutched the railings from the dark side of the cellar. Her curled fingers were bony and white. Her skin seemed stretched over her frame making her appear ghostly. One of her white calves appeared between the rails.

"Ain't you got some food for a poor old woman?" She smiled and as I became accustomed to the dark I saw that she did not have many teeth.

I held out the tray with several chunks of the brown meat and she snatched one from a plate. I could hear her sucking and swallowing and then she spit a brooch of mucus upon the stairs.

"You'll be back for more food soon, dearie. Don't you forget your old friend, Mabel. Lots of 'em do after a while. Pass me by as if I weren't nothing to 'em anymore." She wiped her nose with the back of her hand. She patted a wretched piece of dirty lace that hung from her sleeve and pulled down her bodice revealing the tops of two small knobs of breasts. "Used to like these, they did. What's yer name?"

"Ann."

"Don't argue with 'em I say. Men. I reckon my father didn't call me his little stick for nothing. You married?"

I could smell the drink as she came closer. "No."

"Clever. One ain't enough. You new?"

I nodded, her hand loosened from the railing and she was receding back into the darkness.

"How 'bout a pint next time fer your ol friend Mabel?" She smacked her lips.

At the top of the stairs I looked back down and saw neither rat nor woman. An orderly carrying a basin and towel draped over his arm said, "Meet Mabel, did you?"

"Yes, I am newly at St. Thomas's."

"Don't feed her," he said, disappearing down a hall. "We don't want her clambering up the stairs and frightening the patients again."

I wanted to ask him more about her but I hurried instead to the patient where her friend quietly waited, still applying the rag.

"I've had such bleak memories," the patient gazed at the ceiling then at the columns scattered in the ward, "with only more to come."

"Oh, come now, Rebecca. Such fiddle-faddle as I have ever heard. Be proper. Miss Russell here has brought you some meat and sago. You must take it and get well."

The patient lifted her pale lidded eyes toward me, her cheeks were waxen, her face was smoothed out and whitened as if she was growing younger and more featureless. "You are kind, Miss." She took the food on the plate with slender fingers and set it gently upon the table. Her mattress creaked.

"You must eat," I exhorted her. "The doctor will return soon."

She gave me a quick look, not frightened, disdainful and tired. "So did you see Mabel?"

"Yes," I stammered. "How did you know?"

"She came from a bawdy-house." Then she closed her eyes and lay back upon her pillow. "I should know."

Her friend turned toward me, "Rumor has it that she was with so many of the doctors that she moved clean into the hospital. But after they tired of her she did not move on. One account has her taking up some nursing duties. She now lives near the kitchen with its warmth and smell of meat, soup, bread, and suet pudding."

"I have seen her myself," Rebecca whispered. "But only at night. Hovering above the mattresses of the dead ones."

Another nurse came in, smelling of vinegar and the warm air turned bitter. "I must open a window," I said. "I will return."

And I passed by a nurse at the bed of a man strapped down whose foot was black below the ankle but for his white toes cracked like a vase that had been dropped a long time ago. I breathed in deeply at the window, promising not to forget my eau de cologne next time. I could hear the distant clop of horses' hooves and I caught the odour of grass and damp earth. When I returned, Rebecca Drake's friend was leaving. Her golden hair and lovely skin were burnished like wood newly polished. I plucked a copy of *The Times* to read to the patient but her friend placed it back onto a table.

"She stifled her baby girl just after it was born, while it was nursing," she whispered in my ear, her breath drumming. "She will be going to prison. Her name may yet appear in the newspaper."

"I will just sit by her a while then." I doubted that she was married but had probably taken on the married name. She was not that different from me in that way.

"That would be comforting." And she left, her deep purple dress billowing, her bonnet askew, her boots tapping along the floor.

But when I returned Rebecca's head tossed upon her gray pillow, her eyes were glazed and open. "Rats. The rats they are upon me."

I started to take her hand but that, too, began to flail. Her hands clawed at nothing. The nurse at the man's bed looked over at me and then she stared at a photograph on the wall over her patient of the old St. Thomas's hospital as if she was wistful for a past time. I missed Flo, coming to my side, commenting, helping, and then moving further down the ward. But I imagined her spirit and her words were with me now.

My hand was resting upon Rebecca's blanket when she suddenly sat straight upright in her bed with her eyes wide open, the pupils enormous. "I can't stand these visions anymore. Help me, Miss Russell. I've had a difficult life for too long." I had never heard a woman beg to die and had not considered it before. She rocked the empty air in her arms as if it was a baby. "I need chloroform for my baby's delivery, doctor. It's too painful." She clutched her stomach and screamed loudly.

Dr. Lawrence hurried over and scratched his beard. "Miss Russell, please mix a generous double dose of laudanum for this patient as well as for the amputation in the other bed. Also a poultice for that patient's foot." And he nodded to where the other nurse was sitting.

I scurried down to the kitchen again and did not see Mabel in my haste. The orderlies were emerging to deliver their last prescribed diets. I smelled some eggs and saw mutton that was gristly and gray, tin mugs were clanking against one another on trays. I found some extra bread and milk set aside for the nurses to use. I added carrots and potatoes and made my poultice. My eyes searched about for Mabel as I started up the stairs, but I did not see her anywhere. It appeared that she would be seen when she allowed it. I was relieved. I placed my poultice aside on top of the apothecary cabinet and mixed quite a few grains of opium into the alcohol. I could still hear Mrs. Drake, the patient, screaming. She cried, "She was here. I saw her at my bedside. She is waiting for my food." Then there was silence.

I watched the reddish grains soften and vein the clear liquid, branches spreading to the sides of the two drinking-glasses. I mixed them then with a spoon so that the medicine took on a thinned red colour like blood in water.

I carried the medicines on a tray back to the ward. Rebecca Drake was now quiet and sleeping upon her dulled pillow. Her skin glistened and was white. Her hands were placid and crossed over her stomach. I knew I could not help her with what she wanted because she was no longer in her right mind. Dr. Lawrence stood over her for a few minutes and then left when she did not move and seemed asleep.

I placed the tray upon a table and helped the nurse, whose name I learned was Jane, with her patient's blackened foot. His flesh smelled flooded and rank and sweet at the same time. I applied my poultice hoping he would not cry out or lose his leg. He moaned a bit at its touch. Jane began coughing raggedly. When she stopped she said, "Check his head. He had lice about his person when he came in."

I examined his head but did not see anything. His hair was greasy with oil and dirt. I wondered what thoughts looked like—were they small, dark, and wriggling? Or like spirits, always travelling? It was then that I heard the queer sound of glass breaking nearby. And when I turned, the ward was empty of visitors, only the patients remained, all in their beds. None were moving about much. Jane and I looked at each other and then at the place the sound had come from. Glass was scattered into shards, clear, sharp pieces of an invisible puzzle, on the floor near the table where I had left the tray. The other drinking-glass was sitting, empty and tall, in its proper place upon the tray. At first I thought of Mabel, with her dark scuttling about, flibberty-gibbet, here, there, and everywhere—her search for food and drink could have lead her here. Jane and I began to pluck up the broken glass. The pieces were jagged and lightweight and airy in our palms like birds about to fly off somewhere. It was then that I noticed a reddish liquid trail to Rebecca's bed. A reddened footprint.

Although she appeared to be sleeping, I lifted up her hand and gloved it with mine. "Did you break the drinking-glass of laudanum, Mrs. Drake?" I asked her gently.

"Only in setting the second one back," she whispered between dry, pale lips. "Tell Mabel there is nothing left for her here." And she turned her miserable head and closed her startled and weary eyes.

I allowed her hand to fall from mine. A fly came and alighted upon the edge of her sheets, reminding me somehow of Hera, although smaller and more dark and nervous. Jane wiped up the spilt medicine and came to the bedside and stood there. The fly trembled and left.

"This being only a fortnight since I started working and all,

I do not want to tell Dr. Lawrence," she uttered.

"Nor do I on my first day here." Rebecca Drake's head pressed deeply into the pillow, her lips were slightly parted as if she were about to speak. I did not like gazing upon the faces of the dead or, in Rebecca Drake's case, the nearly dead. "We shall keep this between ourselves then." For we knew she would be gone soon. Jane nodded. "I will fetch more medicine for the remaining patients."

I felt a pull above my heart, quite like a pain, for my mistake. It should not have happened and I was not diligent. I did feel terrible that she had ended her own suffering whereas she could have recovered and lived to have other children. I will only mind the hopeless and there were many of them during the war. But this was a mistake and should not have happened, no matter what the outcome of any trial she may have been made to bear. She was the first woman to die even vaguely by my hand. And I wondered for a moment whether I regretted more that it should have been my hand that had offered her the drink, my hand to have made the decision, rather than the act itself. She had been the first patient to outwit me and I did not want to doubt my nursing skills. But we were past any determinations.

"I will go," I said. "You may tend to your patient's foot." I felt the weight of something heavy hung about my neck and thumping against my heart. To knock it down or be allowed in. I thought of her friend's face when I would have to tell her that her dear friend was gone.

In the apothecary cabinet I moved the ipecacuanha wine and paregoric elixir out of the way. Glass was tinkling against glass. Light shone through the cabinet displaying all the reds, blues, greens, and golds that comprised the medicines. Stump pillows for the amputees that the nurses had made sat obediently underneath the cabinet like small, fat pets. I closed my eyes for a minute thinking of all the amputations, hemorrhages, and gangrene that the war produced at Scutari—cases that were either well or dead within three weeks. When I looked at my two drinking-glasses streaked with the opium grains in a pattern that resembled red lightning or a red storm about to appear, I caught sight of two white calves rubbing against one another at the side of the cabinet. Looking higher, there was the same tattered dress and worn chemise. Her bony fingers clutched the corner of the cabinet and inched closer. Only now I saw her wild, whitened hair and her face and mouth sunken around her bones. Her eyes dipped in and out of the shadows, seesawing, blinking. A ghost leaving darkness behind her, her countenance was close to me, bird-like and angular, jutting toward me. Her bony finger tapped at my shoulder.

"It's all right," Mabel said. As though I needed comforting.

~

I stumbled upon a Roman Catholic church on my way home toward the Thompson house and entered it. The fitful light and coloured glass, the same colours as in the apothecary, matched my own heart. I had never set foot in a Roman Catholic Church before. I did not like doubt and hoped God would agree with me. My father had been a non-believer and my mother cared only for the religion that helped her to receive the most number of invitations to parties. Flo had had terrible rows with the nuns, since they often converted patients upon their deathbeds. I wanted to think about repentance. Instead,

I watched men and women cross themselves as they entered and sat in the pews. I heard some wailing in the penitence box and unintelligible words uttered in a singsong manner. A man reeking of too much drink was escorted out by a priest who held him by the ear. I could hear him cursing. Panes of glass directed their coloured light in patterns over the unhappy pair. Broken pieces of light skittered on the walls. The hard pews, the huge cross hung dead center, the sound of people muttering prayers to themselves and to the others they hoped would listen. Asking for help seemed somehow reassuring.

I thought of Martin and Flo and felt little repentance concerning them. But Rebecca Drake had died because I had looked away too long. Albeit by her own unhappy hand. I could not be certain it was my fault. Perhaps, I told God, if I did some good deed to make up for it, it would be better. But He did not answer me. Again, even here. And I knew I would need to answer myself. I kneeled just as I saw others do. I vowed to do a good deed without determining what it should be. Just that I would know it when I saw it. And, in some manner, I was answered by a wafer slipped onto my tongue, a sip of wine. But I still heard nothing in reply except for Latin in the church. Flo had said that when God came to her those three times, at her family house in Embley, also in Egypt, telling her to be a "savior," they were outdoors, not in a church. So it was something I believed I must try, out in nature, speaking to Him. For I did not know how to grow closer.

I returned my Bible, gathered fistfuls of my skirt, and entered the sunlit street. A horse stumbled along the road, fell, and then righted itself. People eddied around it. The van it pulled lurched a bit and then continued on. I decided to walk since it was a pleasant day outside and would, perhaps, disperse my gloomy thoughts. And, in doing so, I felt nearer to Him. I wondered that in asking God's approval, in seeking His permission, was it not the same thing as asking my father or some other man to sanction my calling? When it had always been my calling alone. And then I hated Him, realizing that, again, it was my own fault, that it was myself that I should be hating.

A small, brown bird perched upon a window sill and jumped at its reflection. On my way to the Thompson house I caught the scent of some yellow flowers pushing themselves up from the soil outside a house. And I thought that with the aid of light and earth and water they, too, would blossom into their calling. That they moved beyond what they were given and became what they were meant to be. As I blinked, outside the yard, the sunlight against the lids of my eyes, I saw the colours of the church's windows, the medicinal colours. And I was not so afraid. For who would know?

It was the time when clocks chimed, carts rattled from the market, carriages ran quickly, and people hurried home. All was suspended between where it had been and where it was going. I found myself in dark, empty, grimy, labyrinthine alleyways near the Thames. For London was older and so much larger than the Nottingham town, where everyone knew me, near my father's house. I held a handkerchief briefly over my nose as the smell from the river was abominable. I found myself mired, ankle deep, in mud upon one street. On another ill-humoured street I heard whimpering behind some refuse, below a dimly lit window. It was a tiny brown dog whose back was torn and its legs broken. It snarled but did not seem to mean it. It rested its head for it could not move. I looked and there was no one about. I broke its neck swiftly, hearing the short snap, leaving it there lying peacefully. And I again felt some satisfaction.

~

At the Thompson's door Mary glanced at my filthy boots and put her finger to her lips to shush me. The blue sky was beginning to darken behind me, and Mary's filmy, curled hair lit up against a wall. "They're trying to call the spirits tonight in the dining room. They're awaiting the night, Miss."

When I looked at her askance, she replied, "It's a dark circle." She watched my puzzled face and realized I knew nothing about these things. "A seance. A famous spirit medium is here, at the head of the table. It was Mrs. Thompson's idea."

"What should I do, Mary?"

"Take them boots off and change and refresh yourself and join the circle. Those were Mrs. Thompson's instructions. They have six people there now and are in need of a seventh according to Mrs. Tatterspol, the spirit medium. But they're waiting for night anyhow. Would you like a maid, Miss Russell, to help with your dress?"

"Yes, just this once," I said, realizing that I would need my velvet dress for Mrs. Thompson's company and it had been a tiring, long day.

"I'll send someone."

In the bedchamber my eyes flickered over Martin and his usual, serious expression. I was tiring of his whiskers, his scornful eyes. I could not read his face, never having really known him. I could feel an ache in my head surfacing near my rag-tag hair. I threw some cool water from a basin upon my face and began my toilette and in doing so discovered a bloom of blood staining my under things. As I stared at the stain it seemed to grow. I used some rags I had brought as I dressed hurriedly. When the maid knocked and entered I was in my gown and merely needed help with the buttons. I thought that I might use a pessary, or a pisser, to hold the blood if I needed to. At the child-sized dressing table draped in pink fringe I used my hairbrush, pomade, lip balm, and a cologne that smelled of lavender and honey to disguise the iron odour of blood that leaked from my body.

The maid had completed her duties. "Anything else, Miss?"

"No, thank you." I had not noticed her before. She curtsied and left.

As I descended down the stairs towards the dining room I thought that I smelled as though I had recently killed someone and had covered it up with cologne. But when I entered the room it was dark and it took some time before I made out Mrs. Thompson and James and a garish woman wearing too much jewelry at the head of the table. Phosphorised oil in jars burned away some of the night, turning it bluish. There was another couple whose faces appeared to float above the already familiar table. A woman sat where Mr. Thompson had died a short time ago. I could barely discern her blonde hair tightened about her head like a luminous ribbon.

"This is Miss Russell," Mrs. Thompson announced. "She is a nurse tending to my illnesses and helping Dr. Lawrence at St. Thomas's hospital."

"Ah, a woman of science," Mrs. Tatterspol at the head of the table said. A blue stone necklace and several bracelets rustled against her bosom and arm. She was older, and yet wore a flowing dress surrounded by much jewelry, her black, crimped hair faded into the surrounding darkness. "Are you also a believer in the spirit world, Miss Russell?"

"I do not think that I believe in any other world than this one." I believed myself to be practical. I would not tell her about the Roman Catholic Church or my attempt to reach Flo's God. Perhaps it was Flo and not the divine I wanted to be closer to. I sat down at the table. I looked at James, doubting that he would believe in a spirit world.

"Are you at least open to the possibility that there are spirits near to us? That there are messages that they mean us to have and that there is truth in spiritualism?"

I did not know what she meant to do—bring Mr. Thompson back to this very place where he had died to speak to Mrs. Thompson? So he could pinch the servants? So Mrs. Tatterspol could perform some parlour tricks? To frighten or enlighten us? "Yes, I suppose it is possible." And I thought that it was not so different from trying to speak to God except that with the spirits we had seen their earthly bodies, and known them through them.

She smiled. "The women must remove their gloves." The women all fell silent and began to peel each glove, rinds that revealed white, delicate hands laced with thin, blue, knobby veins. Our fingers perched uselessly on the table between us or tangled upon our laps. My own hands were chilblain and dry from my recent nurse's work and the constant cleaning. To me she said, "Miss Russell, we are much alike." She stopped and fidgeted with the blue necklace. "I have helped many women, and men also, that were unwell with irritations, nervousness, insomnia, stomach ailments, and pains in their joints. And I am sure you have done the same." And she nodded at me.

"Yes," I said, my hands turning, pale as fish upon my lap,

"but I am certain our methods are different."

"Miss Russell helped the soldiers during the Crimean War," Mrs. Thompson stated.

"And she was never the same when she returned," James mumbled, but I overheard him.

"I may be able to aid you with that, Miss Russell," Mrs. Tatterspol said, "and any nightmares you may still be experiencing."

"I am perfectly well," I replied. "What are we to do now to attract the spirits?" I could see Mrs. Tatterspol's eyes and lips and blue jewelry wavering in the dim light.

"Take the hand that is next to yours." And everyone did so except for our spirit medium.

I held the man's hand from the couple. His grip was hard and tight, his skin was roughened like brushstrokes, long and dry and ridged upon a painting. The blonde woman's hand was soft and open in my palm. Then we closed our eyes and after several minutes we heard raps upon the table. Mrs. Tatterspol asked us to sing several hymns. We sang all the verses we knew and waited.

"I shall see if any spirits come," she said mysteriously.

We sat for about fifteen minutes and then our medium appeared to go into a trance, her eyes opened and their whites showed, her lips quivered without making a sound. Her black hair danced upon her head in the bluish half-light. I had seen patients having mild fits before like this one. A yellow flower suddenly materialized upon the table near Mrs. Thompson.

"Does this flower have any significance to any person here?" Our medium's voice trembled. There was silence as we stared at its luminous petals.

Finally the woman of the couple spoke. "It is our anniversary flower, a daisy."

"Yes, yes," our spirit medium's voice growled, grew deeper. "I have a message. Bring me paper and pen. But do not in any circumstances break the circle. It is important." Her face changed, her body grew larger, her gestures different as her hands twisted in the air. "Ah, who has called me?" She rubbed her chin. "My, it is an interesting group here that has called me. There are many handsome ladies." Her head swiveled about the table but her eyes were shut tight. Her accent and voice and body seemed all changed. "Did you save any food or drink for me?"

"No, we are sorry, spirit," the blonde woman to my side answered.

"What is it that you would like to know of me?" The low voice from Mrs. Tatterspol asked.

"How is it where you are?" James inquired rather politely.

"I am in one of the seven spheres, a low one or new one for spirits. Where I am it is calm and bright and there are many other spirits here. Some are willing and even anxious to talk to you even though they have recently departed."

"Is my husband there?" Mrs. Thompson burst out.

"Yes," the deep voice from Mrs. Tatterspol's body said. "He said he has left you with many material things on earth and that you and your son will be well cared for. He has inquired about your health and suggested that you try the water cure again, eat brown bread and vegetables and apples in abundance. And try quinine."

"What does my father say about my upcoming marriage?" James smiled a crooked smile even in the darkness.

"That it shall be an especially difficult marriage." Mrs. Tatterspol grew limp, draping her chair with her limbs, and then stiffening again. "Another spirit is approaching," she said in her own voice. This one was female, for her gestures were light and airy and her head tilted to the side slightly. Her breath quickened as though she was breathing for two people.

"Who is there?" The other gentleman to my side asked.

"My spirit name is Ariel." Mrs. Tatterspol opened her eyes but they were shiny and pulsing and unformed, a slightly younger woman's eyes. She stared. "I am happy here. Why have you requested my presence? Is it your own guilt?"

I cringed. "If I offered you wine where would it go when you have departed from the medium's body?" I inquired, trying to ascertain bodily evidence, some kind of proof.

"It would be found in Mrs. Tatterspol's stomach." Her movements seemed gentler than the medium's, no bracelets jingling or earrings swinging, slow as water.

I felt Hera's presence again, swooping low as if to pick up some piece of food. A brief, white flapping of wings. I wanted her to ride my shoulder or eat from my fingers again. But she was quickly gone. My witness.

"Where is my little boy? Do you see him?" The woman next to me called out. "He has pale, daffodil-coloured hair, a sweet smile."

"Yes, he is here and there are angels about him and he has his dear hand about mine and wants you to have a kiss." Our medium rose up and went to the woman whose hand I held limply in mine and placed a kiss upon her cheek. Her head hung down against her chest and she squeezed my fingers tightly as she cried loudly. Her blonde hair loosened and was wetted down with tears.

"He is my own loving boy." The medium stroked her damp cheek.

"Can you see my brother who died when we were children?" The gentleman on my other side asked, his face leaping toward the oil jars, his eyes wide.

"Did he have whitened hair?" Mrs. Tatterspol's eyelids flickered, her mouth grew thinner.

"Why yes. It grew white too early on. He was so sick and frightened. That is him."

"He says to tell you to view the whole shape and meaning of social and political events, to go beyond their outer shells. Look to their inner concerns."

"Thank you."

His hand had become relaxed in mine. The blonde woman was still crying onto the table, her arms outspread, her fingers still cupped within mine.

"I hate it that you have requested my presence so soon. I like being far away, from anyone's touch, from all earthly goings on," Ariel's voice said. Our medium stood in her chair again and began rocking her arms as if she held a baby there. "Such a little thing to be with me again."

"Alice, my Alice, my sister," the woman from the couple cried. "And the baby."

But I did not believe her.

The whole dark circle watched her elbows, her sleeves pushed up a little, exposing her bare arms. Her bracelets remained quiet upon her wrists. "For the one here who is bleeding, do not punish yourself any longer, I am in my rightful place. You must find yours." And then Mrs. Tatterspol's arms went slack and the rest of her body followed as if she suddenly fell asleep. Her sleeves fell down and the bracelets rested intertwined. Her eyelids fluttered and then opened to reveal her brown eyes. Her lips grew plumper and she sat up in her chair. "Did the spirits pass among you and answer all your questions?"

"Yes," we murmured and nodded all six of our heads towards her one.

I, for one, was relieved that the spirits, if that was what they were, were gone.

"What was it like being ordered about by a spirit?" The wife in the couple asked.

"It was as if I had been emptied out and put aside and another self had come and possessed me, as though I was a chair to be filled or an empty page to be written upon."

"It seems so strange. Where do you go?"

"I do not know. I seem to be floating above."

"You are so brave."

And on their way out each person left several pounds upon an embroidered handkerchief bearing Mrs. Tatterspol's name. I did not. I did not enjoy the unpleasant performance and did not want it repeated but could not say so in front of Mrs. Thompson. Mrs. Thompson spoke to Mrs. Tatterspol about private sessions, their heads tilted together with nearly touching foreheads. In the greater light I could discern her rouged cheeks and darkened eyes, her too black hair, her bright jewelry and ample figure.

*My Dearest,*

*Our children have grown up and taken their own lives. It happened at St. Thomas's hospital—on my first day there. A woman, a prostitute or former one, I believe. She took her own life—as she had taken that of her newborn child's, as if her life was a pair of unfit gloves or an unattractive frock to be discarded. Too lightly. But it was* my error for leaving the means out for her to attain her goal. Mine more than another nurse who was present also. I do not think she was dying. She simply did not want to continue on. May God forgive me—for I am not certain that I can forgive myself for such a gross mistake. Perhaps you can ask God to forgive me—for I do not have a relationship with Him. Yet. And the woman has already come and visited me—unlike Martin, one of the soldiers that died in the Crimea, or any of the other dead—through a spirit medium—I hope she will not haunt me. I cannot imagine the specter of her rocking her child returning again and again. The only good is that I glimpsed Hera again in the spirit room and I do miss her, as I am sure that you miss Athena. I do wish that I had your faith.

I feel some nervousness coming on—similar to the episodes at Scutari and I shall take some chloral to calm my nerves and for sleep. For I need to be alert at the hospital. I wish I could hold your hand for strength, gaze into your gray eyes for endurance. I do miss my father terribly and wish he had been the one to come to me instead of the prostitute who died.

I have received letters from my mother and sister and they said that in three months time they want me back home so that we can all visit the Lucan household at Hampshire. Nothing could be duller, except that they have a magnificent garden there with mazes that I cannot find my way out of without shouting. Both my mother and sister still wear black two years after my father's death but they attend many parties that their lives center upon.

I will try and repair my relationship with James as I have attempted to with God—for both are difficult. I will then count that as my repentant act to remedy my own guilty nursing mistake—if I am successful.

*I would like to see you and clear up our small misunderstanding.*
*I think of you often.*

*Yours Truly*

## At the Thompson House

"Did you know, Ann, that I had been to a medium before?"
James faced the fire in the drawing room and his profile glowed
orange, his legs stretched onto the rug whose dark border was
knotted with light. The fire grate misplaced his nose and mouth
with shadows when his head rotated toward me. His arms
rested, content upon the thick chair. Candles worked some
light into the shell design carved along the chair legs making
the wood appear nearly aflame, flickering and nesting around
protuberant spots. The doilies spread about took on a look of
sinister spider webs. The firelight grazed our clothes, fussed
with our hair and the walls of the room. It sizzled. James was
not unattractive as his reddened blonde hair touched his cheek
after a dash of light departed.

"No, I did not know." I warmed my hands at the fire.

"I believed that they were all about tricks before then. I had
heard about rolling a cone from plain paper to make their voices
queer and carry, or women that used pins in their hair to write
out messages along their flesh. That was before I was roused
from my bed to write messages one night. My arm twitched
for the pen and paper and a spirit whispered words to me that
were not my own. Base and filthy words that I burned when
the writing was over."

"When was this, James?"

"Almost six years ago."

"Before or after you asked me to marry you?" My fingertips were gloved in warmth, were holding onto the heat.

"Afterwards. And it did not happen again. Thank goodness."

"Yes, thank goodness." But I did not care about his suffering, for he knew nothing of mine.

"My hands were not my own but were puppets of some
terrible spirit. I am pleased that it never happened again. I do
not know how Mrs. Tatterspol endures it."

"I cannot imagine you unable to tell your arms and legs
what to do." I gazed at my hands which I hoped healed the
sick as fiercely as any medium's. And healing took on many
various forms.

"It was terrible, but it is done now."

"Your mother has not told me about your fiancé."

"I do not have one as yet." He poked at the fire making the
flames quicken and leap into the shapes of new spring shoots
and flowers. "I was testing Mrs. Tatterspol."

"Perhaps she saw the wife you shall have." I was indiffer-
ent but would make an effort toward repentance.

"Perhaps." He stood behind his chair with his arms braided along the back. "I suppose you were hoping to hear from
Martin at the seance. Anyway, are you still married to your
nursing?"

"Yes, it is what guides my life." I narrowed my eyes to the
flames and saw a bright, orange lake. "What business are you
involved with, if I may ask?"

"It is very interesting. Have you heard of Michael Fara-
day?"

"Yes, he recently died."

"Yes. I know a friend of his who is working on electricity and magnetism. The electromagnet. I am helping him."

"There are so many unseen forces working all around us. Electricity and magnetism and spirits. It seems we are pushed and pulled greatly by them."

"You cannot see anger or love. Why be able to see electricity?"

"We cannot see what makes people sick either." Or God, I thought.

"It appears we see only a small part of the world," he said. "But with this invention of electricity, just think of all we could see if it is harnessed correctly." And he moved into the shadows, his blonde hair becoming dark brown.

"It is nice to see you so animated about your work. When we were children together you were not always so proper."

"My mother taught me early on that you cannot drink from a cup that has overflowed. You must first clean the spill and then fill it properly." He rubbed his hands together.

"Perhaps we can discuss this Darwin I have heard so much about sometime."

"I can lend you his book, On the Origin of the Species. We can discuss evolution and natural selection." And then he laughed heartily—I did not know why.

As I moved from my chair toward the door James made to take my arm and instead he tugged a dark strand of my hair out of place. It coiled along my neck and collar, tickling me.

"Did you tell your mother that you had asked me to marry you several years ago?"

"No, I do not share much with her. I had asked you without thinking." He stood away from me. "I knew that she would have approved."

"I am sorry that my heart is still threaded with Martin."

"Yes, Pain, we are often like brother and sister now."

He pulled at the loose hair and tugged at my scalp so hard that my head lifted. "I must go and rest so I can cure the sick of their unseen infections and fevers tomorrow." I pulled my hair away from his fingers and did not say a word, remembering my repentance. Then I angrily mustered my way through the door.

~

Mary, who had stayed at the open door to the drawing room while James and I talked, inquired if I wanted my hair brushed or help with my gown. "Any more food from the kitchen, Miss, after your long day?" When I told her no, she handed me a shining lamp to carry as I climbed the stairs.

But when I arrived at the top of the stairs I heard Mrs. Thompson's voice calling to me, "Ann, Ann. Is that you at the door?"

I hesitated and then thought that this would be another good deed, for James was not too unpleasant. Each person had their own view of what a selfish act was—to Flo it was being vain or being too involved with the self—for James it was excluding others in business—for Mrs. Thompson it was being sick and having others tend to you. And for me? Not helping the truly suffering. I wondered whether these would change as the years went by.

"Yes. May I enter?"

Mrs. Thompson was upright in her bed, her bonnet worrying her eyebrows, her bedclothes rumpled beneath her lacy coverlet. Darkness muscled the room, spread deeply into the corners. Her lamp's light crept up her wall, pooled around her plump face and shoulders. I placed my lamp next to hers on the table and they flickered at one another as if engaged in a conversation.

Her eyes glistened. "Mrs. Tatterspol was wonderful—was she not? I am now able to discuss important financial matters with Mr. Thompson at a time when it is so necessary. James does not listen to me. I am so excited to begin private sessions with Mrs. Tatterspol this week. Why, did you see how moved the guests were to see their loved ones again?" She rushed her words.

"I believe she is comforting to many people, Mrs. Thompson, but it is difficult to know whether the information she imparted was correct, whether she is really in contact with the departed." Even in the poor light I noticed a nest of veins rise and tangle in her right cheek.

"Oh, that was certainly Mr. Thompson. She even resembled him. And I do need to speak to him." She fussed with her blankets and bedcovers, her knuckles and fingers were all knotty.

"I cannot imagine that the spirit world is still that interested in this one." I wanted to say that the spirit world could bear too greatly upon me, that I was comfortable with the dead being gone—except for missing my father.

"Oh yes. But many have left too much undone and these matters need fixing." She was becoming agitated.

"I will fetch you a draught of laudanum so you will get some rest." Thoughts raced wildly across her face, changing in the whims of light each time I looked at her. Wind knocked at her window.

I mixed a dose for myself also, moving aside the carbonate of soda and cough pills in my wooden medicine chest to make more room for the extra laudanum. After I gave Mrs. Thompson her laudanum she murmured something about fetching her Chinese dog which I ignored.

But when my head rested finally upon my pillow I wondered whether I hid from complications the way Mrs. Thompson did, merely in a different manner. I dreamed that Hera's sweet beak and great, open eyes lay against my cheeks and neck, protecting me. Her soft feathers stirred against my jaw and I stroked a tuft near her wing. I hoped she would never leave me again. And then a great crack of lightning frightened us with its noise and electrical light, scattering us, and I lost sight of Hera in my dream.

~

The morning light pitied me and collected around a glass lamp painted with daffodils and blades of grass. Light molded around the glassy skin of the window. Then pierced right through it. I opened my eyes. It was early and I felt rested, my eyelids fluttered, inviting full knowledge of the day. My bedsheets were scattered about my person as though I had been too warm in the night. Several moths lay inert outside my window, along the sill. They had detected my bright lamp last night and attempted to get too close or they mistook the light for the moon, a fatal mistake. I laughed, wondering whether God could see things my way.

I dressed myself unhurriedly and tiptoed downstairs. No one else was about except for Mary and the other servants bustling to and from the scullery and dining room, anticipating breakfast. Mary poured me some tea and I ate heartily of coddled eggs, cold salmon, and bread. I would not have known that there was a seance in this room except for the warm air sharpened by the smell of a wilted flower that had been recently removed. All else seemed orderly, nothing too frilly-dilly about plates and saucers whose bands of gold circled my food. Or the tepid tea that had probably been sitting in the kitchen for hours, becoming stronger and more bitter with time. Like the spirits, I thought, becoming bored and vengeful the longer it had been since they left their bodies and forgotten what it was to have one. Excepting the use of a medium's. How difficult it must be to give a body up once they had used it for their purposes, imbibing tea or drink, or stealing a kiss. Unless they found a measure of happiness in the place where they now resided. For presently I needed to be off to tend to the bodies that were still here—the ones merely missing an arm or leg or racked with an infection or a fever.

~

When I arrived at the hospital Jane was coughing by the bed of the man with the blackened foot. He appeared to be insensible, his head rolling, his eyes fitful, his remaining skin was the colour of tapioca pudding, making the cracked, dark, swollen foot more noticeable.

"He is broken, Ann, and I don't know what to do." She coughed into the spaces between her fingers on the back of her hand.

Dr. Henry Lawrence appeared at the bedside, rubbing his beard and frowning. "It must come off," he exclaimed. "Prepare this man for an amputation, Miss Russell."

But it was Jane I had to prepare. We brought out a screen to place around the bed. I closed my eyes and saw the thin mattresses at the Scutari barracks alive with vermin that crawled across my book like words and raced over my hands. That was before Flo scrubbed the rotting wood underneath and cleaned everywhere. I was relieved when Dr. Lawrence asked for chloroform, which Dr. Hall did not believe in using at the Crimea. Jane went to fetch the chloroform and I went henceforth to the kitchen for water. The stairs creaked on my way down and in the distance I believed I saw a pair of eyes shining at me. I could not tell if they were human but they were curious as to whether I carried food. I noticed a thin, white powder scattered about the floor and then the rats teeming over one of their own. I descended quietly lest they should discover me or understand their probable fate. Mabel's tense, white hand flung itself upon the railing as I was ascending. She wore the same dress and her hair and shoulders were dusted with white powder as if she wore a veil. She looked about her miserably, her fair skin contrasted with the scurrying darkness behind her.

"I see you minded the stairs. Good. Got anything for me?"

I shook my head. It was early in the morning still. Her breath stank of drink and made the air foul between us. She touched my hand with a bony finger. I nearly withdrew my hand but kept it upon the railing by force of will.

"I can't stay here much longer, Miss Ann, or I'll be poisoned too." And she looked behind her, white powder dusting the walls and the backs and tails of rats.

"Let me see what I can do," and I removed my hand and summoned my courage to continue up the stairs.

The sweet, fruity smell of chloroform emanated from the patient as Jane pressed a pad over his nose. I had not forgotten my lavender perfume today and it mixed with the chloroform vapors giving the ward a strange flowery and springtime odour throughout. When Dr. Lawrence brought forth a saw and the other surgical instruments I thought Jane would faint dead away. But she proved to be a good nurse and helped Dr. Lawrence with the unnerving task and blood that rushed to cover her apron and sleeves. An orderly fitted the foot in a large basin and hurried it away from the eyes of the other patients that felt well enough to be curious.

Afterwards, when Jane and I changed our aprons I noticed a twitch in her eye. "I like him," she said still coughing. "I hope he'll be well again."

"We will do our best, shan't we, Jane?" But I knew it was hard to predict. I had seen men with surface wounds die quickly while a man who lost two legs reached home. "I saw Mabel downstairs."

"That's not a good omen."

"She said that she needs to leave here. They are poisoning the rats near the kitchen."

"She certainly needs another life. Perhaps the workhouse?"

I tried to imagine Mabel sleeping in a tray-bed, displayed like a present in a box, someone snoring into her face. The large, open room with one small washroom. She would be happier sharing her space with animals as she did now. That much I understood about her.

"I heard that she used to be a nurse here. Dreadful how we can end up," Jane wiped some blood from her boot.

I did not want to mention what I had heard of her former life. I began scrubbing the floor for the second time that day. I watched as my wrists made large circles, invisible designs upon the ward floor.

In Rebecca Drake's former bed was a sleeping man covered

to his neck by blankets, a hand missing two fingers rested above
his hidden stomach. His hair was dust-coloured and winged
about his pillow. His side-whiskers were reddened. His mouth
drooped like a flower picked and left too long. Dr. Lawrence
was soon by the patient's side, checking for a fever or any other
conditions that needed remedying. The patient's visible hand
flew to Dr. Lawrence's neck and gripped him hard there. When
I blinked my eyes I saw the medicine-coloured glass windows
in the church. Then Jane and I rushed to Dr. Lawrence's side
and pried off the man's remaining three fingers.

"I was trying to see if you were mending," Dr. Lawrence
sputtered, uncharacteristically ruffled, testing his throat and
voice. He twisted his head to and fro.

"Sorry," the patient said. "I was in the Crimean War and
believed you were a soldier trying to steal my clothes while I
was sleeping." His eyes were green and striped with black like
miscoloured bees and they flew about the room, determining
where to alight, what place he had just awakened in.

"Why, Miss Russell here was also in that war as a nurse.
Perhaps you saw her there?"

"I would have remembered her had I seen her there." He
moved his errant arm to his hip. "I did see 'The Bird' and remember her among the dysentery and diarrhoea cases."

I sat by his bedside and took his damaged hand. It was
smaller than it seemed, the fingernails were those of a child,
the missing fingers left jagged, stumpy joints. I wanted to speak
to him of Flo when suddenly Rebecca Drake's friend came in
with feathers bristling upon her hat and a parasol with white
trim by her side. She searched the ward for her friend and then
came to her friend's bed. She removed her gloves and I took
her hand instead and we sat in a corner where morning sun

congested next to a painted urn with a plant whose leaves trellised the wall. And as I told her that her friend was gone her face wettened and then hardened and she asked, "How?" She held onto my hand and gently and without thought separated each finger.

When I told her that her friend had died because of infection and fever, her features softened and her body sighed, "She escaped her bleak memories and fate at last." I patted her hand, yet she held mine and traced the rough edges of my knuckles.

"The rest of us are now left with new ones," she said to our skirts.

I asked her what she would like to do with the body and her blue eyes brimmed over again and I thought that I would drown in her tears and probably ought to. "We worked together and shared rented rooms." She gazed at our entangled hands, a tear staining her cheek. Behind her an engraving of one of Raphael's Madonnas dipped in a red dress and lovingly held a child. The Madonna's head bowed at an angle similar to this visitor. Both women were engaged with their pasts, holding them, full of sympathy and love. One I hoped would look forward to the future. It was then, at a vulnerable and empty time, that I asked her whether she would like to take Mabel under her wing.

She recoiled. "It would be as if inviting death into one's home."

"She is filthy also," I added. "And homeless. But I cannot leave her here amidst the rats and poison."

"She is nothing to you."

"That is true."

"I shall consider it, although she is nothing to me. I may be able to change her for the better although that is no small task." She wiped her tears upon her sleeve. "I shall go to the dead-house now." The Madonna looked upon her disappearing, undulating hat with kindness.

After she had gone Dr. Lawrence said that she had seemed to have taken her friend's death fairly well.

"As well as can be expected," I replied. For he had seen many women crying. The men were usually quieter in their suffering. "I have asked her if she can help Mabel, who cannot abide the rats and poison any longer and I do not know how she shall live."

"There are many Mabels," he said. "You have gone too far asking that woman to help her. Why not take her in yourself?"

"I live temporarily at a friend of my family's and cannot ask them to accommodate her."

I saw Jane's uneven eyes peering at me from above the chest of a patient; her neat dark hair fell across her aquiline nose. She coughed and her hair flew. "You cannot ask someone to do something that you cannot do yourself," Dr. Lawrence said.

And I knew he was wrong about that but did not say so, there on the ward with patients watching us. For who else would one ask? I was asked many times but I would not tell him about that.

I dilly-dallied about, straightening sheets and pillows, filling glasses of water, checking medicines, retrieving a new stump pillow for the patient whose foot was healing, threading my way back toward the veteran. He was now reading The Times. He allowed it to drift to the floor, crumpling in the air, when he saw me approaching.

"A man in Sweden named Alfred Nobel has recently invented a new substance called dynamite."

"It has a frightening name. What does it do?"

"It's an explosive that can blast a hole in a hill or a mountain or kill about twenty men at once."

"That is what only God may do." For lately I had been considering God's decisions, acquiescence, and limitations.

"Or war," he said, still the soldier.

"I suppose there are many uses for such a thing. Some good and some bad depending upon whose hands it henceforth falls into."

"Yes, such power should only be wielded by the pure of heart. But that is rarely so. I have seen some men changed by their military power over other men. They became...villains." It was not quite the word he wanted. Perhaps he meant evil or merely too political.

A patient began howling and I looked about the large, whitewashed room with painted streaks of coal-dust upon the walls, my eyes skimming the beds. "It is good that people most often do not get what they want, I suppose." Some people, I thought. I grabbed a basin and started off down the ward.

"I remember a soldier to the left of my sick bed dying of cholera right in the middle of a sentence." He waved his lumpy hand.

"I shall return." This was the second time that day that I had to leave off talking to him. The howling emanated from a woman patient laying in her bed who had complained of stomach pains earlier. She was wearing black lace mittens and was knitting, clacking the needles above a patch of a bright green scarf whilst she screamed. She was plump with a tiny bonnet balanced upon her thin hair.

"What is the matter?"

"I am bleeding," she answered in a calm voice. Her pale flesh flung itself rhythmically between the holes of the lace as the needles rose for a stitch. She put her knitting aside and removed one mitten and there remained a pattern upon her hand as if the lace had been etched upon her hand.

I looked above her waist but she appeared fine so I knew it was below. I lifted the covers slightly and the hot, damp, iron smell of blood assaulted me, the odour of mud mixed with an animal's stomach or the inside of a squash left rotting too long. I suspected abortifacients. I peered closely at her knitting needles, discarded now at the side of the bed, but I did not detect any blood. A button of blood seeped through the top cover, a red coin.

She looked at me. "I tried the Infallible French Female Pills and falling down the stairs but neither of those worked. A friend, Elizabeth Donell, told me that Rebecca Drake died here recently after killing her newborn child and I didn't want to end up like her." Her face contorted with the pain.

So that was the beautiful blonde friend's name, Elizabeth. "I shall call Dr. Lawrence."

~

At the Thompson house Mary brought up hot water and tipped it into the china bowl in my washstand so I could wash myself after the hospital and before dinner. The splashing water relaxed me instantly as though all the tension itself poured out of me. Afterwards I watched steam blur my vision of the first leaves on several trees outside the window. The greening square of lawn softened. The new pink flowers became one enormous, smudged pink flower. The world outside grew hazy, merging the way snow unites and hides at the same time. I could gaze upon it for hours, my own private, ever-changing

painting. Alas, the sun would set and the allegations of night
would begin again. Often I avoided dinner at the Thompsons
just as I had at my own house. The dreary conversations, the
important yet immensely boring guests. All that frippery. As a
child I would spend one whole dinner staring at the dark mole
on the chin of a Lord, imagining it to fester into an illness that
I could cure with my nursing knowledge. I thought of the food
moving down the Lord's stomach. Even then thinking of intes-
tines and the busy work of nurses. But I was interested when
the Lord described a health exhibition he had attended that
particular day. "All spit and blood and sanitation. The stalls
were trying to sell odd contraptions and novelties, such as a
folding teepee for sweating out poisons or a fever or special
saffron spices to combat scarlet fever. Excuse me for mention-
ing this at dinner, ladies," he said, stuffing a potato into his
mouth. And I returned to monitoring the progress of his mole
as it flitted up and down as he spoke or ate, resembling a fly
about to take off for someplace more entertaining.

I stared into Martin's eyes as I lathered the oblong, hospital-
smelling, pale yellow soap named "Sylvia's Square of Cleaning
Compound." I had never known anyone less whom I was supposed to love more. I chose a maroon watered-silk dress that
went nicely with my dark hair. The folds in the skirt darkened
to the colour of night caught in the corner of this room. Poor
Rose, Mrs. Thompson's gone daughter, I thought, and I could
hardly remember her. She barely had time to learn the twists
and turns of the house.

When I went down to dinner Mary had just served a watery soup swimming with vegetable pieces and fish. I wondered if they were left over from the previous night's dinner. I
was relieved to discover Mrs. Thompson, James, and myself as

the only diners.

James was saying, "I called at Baker Street today to see Madam Tussaud's Exhibit. My colleagues had told me much about it. Have you ever seen it, Mother?" She shook her head. "Have you, Ann?" I shook my head, no. "She has Joan of Arc, Napoleon, even Queen Victoria there. I heard the Duke of Wellington is a regular visitor who enjoys seeing himself there and comparing the likeness. But it is remarkable—the figures. All made of wax. There was a Grand Hall and a House of Horrors. It is truly incredible. You should visit there, Mother. I felt as though I could reach out and touch the figures, talk to them."

"That Marie Tussaud made death masks of many of her former employers. Often right after they had been to the guillotine. That is what my friend Charlotte told me and I would not set foot in there after hearing that." Mrs. Thompson sipped at her soup. "It would be like Mary making wax models of us after we had died."

Mary continued serving as if she did not hear her name bandied about.

"Oh, but you should see the Sleeping Beauty there. A lovely girl in a froth of pink and blue. Asleep with her arm thrown over her face. She seemed so real—I wanted to touch her hair, her pale, smooth cheek."

"Men," Mrs. Thompson exclaimed, "need their toys and do not heed much else. They are too busy seeing what they can do with them to give much thought as to why they are there to begin with." She put her spoon down onto a plate. "Ann, men need to explain things or play with them rather than truly know them. You are lucky, my dear Ann, that no man has told you who you are yet." She shook her head. "An inert wax figure as lovely as a real woman. One that does not speak at that."

"I would like to go and see these wax figures," I said to James, "as long as it does not resemble being among eerie ghosts on a moonlit night."

"It is more real than that." He turned his spoon over and over on his napkin. "Some are quite well dressed. Unlike most ghosts." He smiled. "I would be glad to take you there." His blonde hair fell forward and fringed his cheek.

Trees clotted the small window in the dining room and seemed to float on their square piece of sky. No clouds or earth were discernable. Just framed trees that appeared to exist on their own. Mary came by with kidney pie and steak. A maid passed by bringing coal upstairs for the bedchambers and parlour.

Mrs. Thompson turned toward me again. "Yet, my dear, a woman needs a man or else she is thought less of than a bar of soap or one of your wax figurines, James. And not any man will do." She plucked a large chunk of meat from the platter Mary was holding aloft. Mary's hair peeped out from her bun. "Mr. Thompson, for example, was a good sort even with his carousing. And Mrs. Tatterspol says he has a good, strong psychic energy."

She did not need to tell me. Mrs. Thompson pulled her black wrap about her large shoulders. She wore mourning dresses even though she was conversing with Mr. Thompson almost every evening, more than she apparently saw him in real life.

"How are your talks with Mr. Thompson?"

"Very well, my dear. He said last night that you had something you needed to inquire of me?" The dark circles underneath her eyes were deep as footprints in mud and were highlighted in the lamplight. Her eyes were round and large. She raised her eyebrows until they created little waves across her forehead.

James was not eating much. He tossed his food from one side of the plate to the other. "Why, yes. I did want to mention my project at the hospital. Her name is Mabel and she is desperate for a place to stay temporarily."

"This is not a hotel." Mrs. Thompson was angry. "Is she sick also?"

"She is a drunk and..."

Mrs. Thompson threw down her fork, clattering, onto her plate. "We have had enough drunks living here." And she brushed past a candle in a whatnot, almost setting herself afire on her way out.

"You are still not very experienced in the ebb and flow of social interaction like your mother or sister, are you, Pain?" He began to eat his food.

I hung my head. "No, and what little I did know nursing has worked out of me."

"Most society women are to be treated as delicately and carefully as fairies and do not want to hear about any earthly indelicacies."

"I get bored with the new fashions, the yellow and orange trains and overskirts, the hip bags, pelisses and capes and tippets. Not to mention the hair pieces and all that goes underneath the clothes. It is so much effort in a frivolous direction."

"Yes, but how is it that you deal with the doctors and the politics of supplies and staffing and shifts?"

"That is different. It is for the greater good of the patients. It is a structure below the structure itself."

He smiled. "You see, Pain, you can do it. Politics is the same no matter where you go. If you are going down a path it is simply a matter of deciding whom you must collide with or not to

arrive at your destination." He finished his rice pudding. "You
would have done better with my mother, handling her more
gently and flattering her, and you know it."

He was correct and I wondered how much I really did
want to help Mabel with her frightening, bony fingers, sunk-
en mouth, and foul breath and I did not know whether she
wanted to continue with her terrible life or truly leave it and
be healed. She was a difficult case. James left and I sat staring
at the white porcelain French clock with blue marigolds dripping from its round edges as the hands moved from one ornate number to another. James had a quicker intelligence and
was less unpleasant than I had remembered. When I thought
of Mabel I wondered whether we were all in our own prisons,
be they marriage, home, work, a hospital, an asylum or simply
within our minds. I needed to ask and answer many questions.
I went upstairs, past Mrs. Thompson's closed door and into her
daughter's room. I knew she would not call for me that night. I
sat at the desk and began again.

*My Dearest,*

*I cannot abide myself some days. I am at an age, a spinster, and
yet I am still able to fool myself and that is a shocking ability. Time is
slippery and, like the trees outside my window, full of tracery, and in
its complications it fools us into believing we understand ourselves—
and sometimes others. But this is not true—because we cannot see
what is roiling underneath and, like an infection, finally makes its
way to the surface. And the surface tells us so little.*

*James and I have mended our relationship—so much so that
he is even dispensing advice to me. Mrs. Thompson is finding more
comfort with a medium than she is with my ministrations.*

*I am attempting to help a woman in the hospital cellar who lives near the kitchen. She is Hera as a worn out woman. She is all white with bony claws, large eyes, and tattered wings and she lives among the rats. She likes drink and perhaps was a prostitute or still is one. Or perhaps she was a nurse and we have known many that liked drink and carousing too well. The hospital is poisoning the rats and she needs somewhere to live, if you know of any such place.*

*I have been too busy to think about the past and that is good..."*

I heard a knock at my door. It was Mary inquiring if I needed help undressing and whether I needed her to fetch my chamber pot. I let her in and exhaled loudly as she undid the buttons along my back—as if I were a balloon that had been loosened. Her hair was haloed against the light from a sconce and I wanted to touch its airiness, it being so fairy-like in contrast to the smooth, hard reality of her cheek. But I did not.

Part II

## Madame Tussaud's Wax Museum

Who was helping whom? I asked myself. It was about comfort. The comfort of Mary's hardworking hands, a lovely house
with servants, free of rats and maggots, the comfort of touch. I
needed to take all into my own two hands. I needed to fashion
myself a life. I was at the hospital watching Jane cradle a once
wretched baby in her arms. She was cooing at the tiny head as
little fists emerged, opening and closing in the direction of the
blossom of her face. I had heard the baby howling inside when
I approached the heavy doors of the hospital entrance that
morning. Her screaming echoed down the corridors, greeted
me as I entered.

Dr. Lawrence whisked the baby past me to examine her.
She was a tuft of red hair and naked skin below his brown
beard. "She was mistakenly left at our front doors this morning."

"The mother must have been distraught," I told him.

Jane fed and comforted the baby as she sat in a straight-
backed chair. "She's a fine, healthy little one. Just miserable
from lack of food. They'll take her to the orphanage later but
now I can treat her like a toff." Jane's coughing was subsiding.
The baby's small, whippy arms knocked a yellowed, misshap-
en doily off of a table. She gurgled and flailed. My own fingers
startled me, like unknown animals, when they poked through

the old lace of the doily I placed back upon the table after cleaning it. Jane held her tight. "I'll call her Carrot for today. See the beginnings of carrot hair, Ann. She's a hard one to give up. So full of energy."

I drifted toward the veteran who appeared to be asleep. One eye opened and he said, "The streets are unsafe. I have heard about meetings that ended roughly and flowed into the streets. I read about one this morning in the newspaper—a work meeting, where the police came and horses ran amuck about the market stalls and carts overturned."

"I know," I said. "And amid all that clatter a baby appears on our doorstep. Carrot we will call her."

"Do you walk home from the hospital?" His sad mouth grew sadder. His three-fingered hand brushed some of his stray hair away from his eyes. Raphael's Madonna seemed to be bent toward our direction and eavesdropping with her head held at a graceful angle.

"Yes, but I am very careful."

"Please, do be cautious, Miss Russell. It is terrible out there." He sat up in bed and his dust-coloured hair covered his reddish whiskers. I could see his uneven teeth and a small white knot of a scar at his neck. The scar blinked at me from underneath his hair. He closed his eyes. "Not to be impertinent, but I can tell when you are coming toward me because there is that smell of lavender that I remember from Scutari. There I could always tell if a nurse was near because there would be a break from the stench."

I sat by his bed, Rebecca Drake's old bed. "So you are recovering here."

"A stab wound from a fight in a pub. Some stevedore from the docks who said the Crimean War was ridiculous and we should have never bothered with the Russians." His greenish eyes sparkled underneath his hair.

"I would have done the same thing if I were a man."

"But you are not. And you need to be cautious, Miss Russell. There are many problems brewing on the streets."

"Yes, but I am merely going to and from my work. I do not have time for much dilly-dallying," I said.

Rebecca Drake's friend, Elizabeth, entered the ward and looked about. But no one that she knew was left. Her golden hair was stuffed into a black bonnet and she wore a mourning dress of a deep black with braids and beads, which rattled slightly and bumped against one another on their strings. She was a stunning woman and vital when not in mourning for one of her friends. She was noticed by everyone. And she appeared to have heard our last exchange.

"Ah, are we discussing Women's Rights here?" She stood behind my chair; one gloved hand rested near my back. "For it is a topic close to my heart and probably yours also, Miss Russell."

I answered, "There are two philosophies prevalent at the moment. One says women should do all that men do simply because men do so, including getting a degree or being a doctor, not because it is the best thing to do. And there is one that says women should do nothing men do, that they should excel at women's work only and therefore be superior in only that. With one it would be said, 'That is wonderful that a woman did that' and the other, 'It is only suitable for a woman.' And does it matter to the woman? She should be doing what her heart and God tell her to do, not act to prove a philosophy only. For it does not matter to the good deeds whether it was a woman that did them or not."

Elizabeth stepped before me and her eyes flashed many colours all at once, darting and scampering around the ward. "But what of the right to obtain a divorce from a husband, the right to own property and make a will, the right to vote? Sir William Blackstone understood the law when he said, 'My wife and I are one, and I am he.' What do you believe then, Miss Russell?" She was tense and rigid with her black arms crossed below her bosom.

"I would like to see economic conditions improve so that there are ample opportunities for education and good and meaningful employment for everyone, especially women." I thought: I am like Flo, I do love women and yet women have been the most difficult group to contend with. I have received little help from them, especially my mother and sister, as well as Mrs. Thompson, in terms of my work.

Her arms fell to her sides as though they were black curtains at the end of a show. Her pale face was flushed into a colour near claret. "As would we all. One must watch for the coxcombries of the human race—be they foolish and conceited men or women. For we women shall win our human rights, shall we not, Miss Russell?"

"What is it you do when you are not here?"

"I am with *The Englishwoman's Journal* in Langham Place. I write some articles and help women find services such as at the Educated Women's Emigration Society, Women's Employment Bureau, or Lady's Institute."

"Are you here about Mabel?"

"Yes, I have decided to take her on. My friends said they would help me with her. And she is a poor, wretched soul and a woman." She gazed at me.

"God Bless you," I said patting her warm, black arm. I

looked about and noticed that Jane had placed Carrot in a basket in the empty bed that the man whose foot we had amputated had resided in. Carrot was quietly sleeping and the ward was silent except for the clatter of instruments in an adjoining room.

"There are not as many patients here today as there were yesterday," Elizabeth said.

By now the veteran had gone to sleep with half of his face hidden in the deep pillow. Or else he feigned sleep. A gobbet of a cigar lay in a cracked dish by his bedside, partially smoked. I did not know how he or his visitor could conceal the smoke from Dr. Lawrence, who did not like it, or the nurses. The hospital linens and blankets were pulled up tightly across his chest. He did not move or speak.

"No." I wondered how many we had lost and I wanted to speak to Jane about the man who had had the blackened foot. "But we have gained little Carrot—at least temporarily." I brushed her dusting of orange hair with my hand as we passed her by. It was sparse and she was bald in most places. "Let us go visit with Mabel and see how she is. I have not had the chance to see her as was my wont to do."

"Do you believe she is still in the cellar?"

"I do not know." I took some candles for safety and they were guttering. Their aberrant light flickered on the faintly greasy handrails so there materialized petals of a polished brown wood as we made our way down the stairs. I thrust my candle forward into the sheer darkness at the bottom of the stairs and I saw tails whipping away, trailing the few rats that were left. Elizabeth's eyelashes seemed to dart as the light blinked. They were in one low position, the light lapped against us, and then her eyelashes scampered higher, mak-

ing the shadows near her eyebrows greater. It was disconcert-
ing that nothing seemed to stay in one place, that everything
changed constantly with the sputtering candlelight. Yet I was
not afraid. Curious, really.

"Mabel? Are you here?" I asked a wall that was lined with
dead rats; a white crust appeared along their sides. Some of
their entrails were visible, perhaps chewed upon. But there
was no answer. I went to the kitchen with Elizabeth following
behind me.

"Has anyone seen Mabel today?" I inquired of a clean-
shaven, young man who was very short, about four-foot and
a half, whose long neck was bent over boiled eggs. His hands
worked furiously.

"No, can't say that I have." He did not stop his chopping or
peer at who was asking. "Maybe she's finally off and run away.
Can't say that I'd be sorry."

When Elizabeth and I stepped backwards, toward the
dank walls outside the kitchen, Mabel was there waiting. She
wore a simple, untorn gray dress, her unanimated, thin hair
was pulled into a bun and her face loomed at us, still sunken
and pale. Her breath smelled of cabbage. Her eyes narrowed
and there was the odour of rotten vegetables from her body. I
instinctively brought my wrist doused in lavender perfume to
my nose.

Mabel's bony fingers grasped my other wrist. "Have you
come to help me out of here?"

I could not fashion my own life but I was trying with Mabel's. I looked at Elizabeth, the kind of woman people made
way for, welcomed to a party, who could sing well and everyone listened. And at Mabel, whom someone would drown so
they would not have to look at her any longer or they would

look past her on a street. I did not want to inquire about her new dress that showed her wrists and ankles. The two women were mismatched terribly. The darkness was punctuated by clattering pots and pans and noises in the kitchen. A basket of light from the kitchen door crouched about our boots, pooled around us.

Elizabeth looked her up and down. "Yes, Mabel. We have come to take you from here but there is much work to do with you and you must promise not to drink or carouse at my house." Her lovely nose tipped toward Mabel.

"I ain't going to the poorhouse. I'd rather stay here." A swirl of gray flew into our faces and Mabel's wrists and fingers pinwheeled beneath our breath.

"There are other alternatives. But you shall only go to the poorhouse, Mabel, if you do not follow the rules in my house." Elizabeth's voice was firm.

"Yes, Miss. I don't know much about the world these days, having spent so long here." Mabel curtsied awkwardly in the cellar, one thin ankle rubbing below the other like sticks trying to start a fire. Her gray skirt spread out in imitation of Hera's glorious wings. Her lank, furrowed hair bowed. It was the worst excuse for a curtsy I had ever seen.

A sickly rat coated in white powder fell upon my boot and tried to gnaw the toe and then crept on, staggering past us. "It is time to go." And I hurried back up the stairs. As I looked back Elizabeth's black gloves and black dress emerged and then the bony, white fingers of Mabel crept up the banister. She held one gray arm with a protruding, pale stick of a wrist across her eyes to block out the sudden light. Beneath, her sunken mouth moved but no words resulted from her lips pressing together and then apart.

Finally she said, "And I ain't been out much during the day." Her naked wrists crossed upon her nose, her feet slithered across the floor.

"And nothing untoward happened to you at night?" I asked.

She laughed then, hard, sputtering some spit between what was remaining of her teeth. I realized it was a ridiculous question.

As we neared the ward I could hear Carrot wailing again, then Jane coughing, the drone of Dr. Lawrence's voice. I was aware of the brisk and unsteady movement of Mabel's naked ankles, the plodding of her feet in a pair of men's laced shoes, Oxfords in what my sister would have named a Balmoral style. Near the door Mabel touched Carrot's cheek and she abruptly stopped her howling, most likely from fright. I said goodbye to Elizabeth and Mabel and took Elizabeth's soft hand in mine, chilblain and roughened from all the hospital cleaning.

"Let me know if you need anything. I would be happy to help."

"I will," she said, half smiling at me and then she gazed at the too pale figure of Mabel in daylight. "I will likely need to call upon you." Her palm warmed my hand. Then she placed her own black wrap about Mabel's shoulders and led her outside the hospital. When I peered out the window there was the beautiful Elizabeth with her hideous shadow, one that would hopefully be remade.

As I turned back toward the ward Dr. Lawrence scooped up Carrot in his arms. "It is time for her to go," he said to Jane.

Jane nudged me and whispered in an ugly fashion, "You should have found a home for Carrot, not that wicked woman."

"What became of the man with the amputated foot?" I finally asked her.

"He died last night and someone took his shoes, nice shoes at that."

~

It was my day off from the hospital and at the Thompson house I encountered the parlour's plush green drapes, the embroidered antimacassar with tassels fitted to the maroon sofa, and crochet mats on well-polished tables that were slipped underneath a cut-glass decanter half-filled with Madeira. Cigars huddled in their boxes and silver candlesticks shone in the light and warmth of Mary's fire. I luxuriated in these goods and chattels that were not mine or my family's but could have been and were so much more than anything my patients had seen. I poured myself a little wine and waited for James, for we were to go to Madame Tussaud's Wax Museum that morning.

Last night I had passed Mrs. Thompson's partly open bed-chamber door and overheard her there with Mrs. Tatterspol. I could hear the clicking of Mrs. Tatterspol's jewelry in the hall, and her low, raspy voice.

"Perhaps tonight he shall disclose what you want."

"I certainly hope so. He did not think so thoroughly about our property when he was alive. I will offer him some drink to enhance his thoughts. Some spirits for a spirit." And they both laughed.

"Or some mutton pie." They laughed again, mumbling about muttons and gluttons. "I cannot say that I have called upon my own dead husband much for advice," Mrs. Tatterspol said. "Yet that has not stopped him from offering it to me."

"I had known Mr. Thompson since he was a young man and trusted his erratic financial judgement. It was difficult to lead him into thinking about financial matters but when I did his advice was quite sound."

"Very well." Most of the candles went out and there was a peculiar hum from the bedchamber. I continued to my own room.

I awoke this morning dreaming that I had a rat around its neck and was squeezing. My hands were stiff and clawed. Later on I inquired whether Mrs. Thompson had slept well since I had not given her any medicines for a while.

"I have been sleeping royally," she replied.

I found it interesting that Mrs. Tatterspol's claptrap provided Mrs. Thompson with a contented mind and I wondered what James thought of it all. I would have to ask Flo what she thought of mediums and seances.

James entered the overheated parlour as Mary was straightening a flowered table-runner. She poked at the roaring fire and I placed my drinking-glass upon a table. I scooped up my beige tippet and draped it upon my shoulders, the ends hanging. I was ready to go. I noticed James' blonde stubbled face, his uncombed hair, and his wrinkled clothes. His vacant, tired, yet impassioned eyes.

"Where have you been?"

"I heard a lecture yesterday at the Royal Academy of Science about amber and cat fur and the Leyden jar and all the electricity generated from them. I have been up all night with my friend attempting to devise a way to harness all that power and energy. To teach it how to do our bidding."

"That is dangerous stuff."

"And heady and exciting also." He curled and uncurled his

fingers, staring at them as if he had never seen them before. "But I did not forget our appointment to go to the wax museum today. Perhaps Mary could fetch me an apple to eat along the way and then we should be off."

Mary rushed from the room. I told him we could wait and see the museum another time but he insisted on going as we had planned. He wanted to see it again. Mary returned quickly holding out an apple all red-skinned with a slight yellow tinge. "Here, Sir."

"Thank you, Mary." And he bit deeply into the apple, exposing its crisp, white interior and its core speckled with black seeds. He ate a quarter of the apple in one bite. He was hungry as well as tired.

We walked. His hair, that smelled sweet and sour and singed, fell into his eyes in clumps. His frowsy clothes inspired me to keep a distance from him. I had not seen him so excitable in many years, since he was a child. The sun was stock still, hidden behind clouds, dozing. The clouds were as ragged as Mabel's dress, gray in a gray sky. The hooves of sturdy horses and the whine and creak of carriage wheels on cobbled roads ribboned our conversation. Perhaps the wax museum could recreate our waxy sky.

"Do you miss your father?" I asked, feeling a tad excitable and pent up myself like the electricity.

"It depends. Little when I think of his carousing with women or drinking too much claret or whiskey." He fiddled with his watch fob. A three-legged dog hobbled by and then ran along the street passing us.

"Not like your mother who really misses him."

"Pain, she misses scheming with him over certain accounts or what to do with our property in the country or Ireland. That is all. Do you miss your father?"

"Yes, he gave us all our own money and I am certainly well enough off because of him but I miss our discussions most of all." A man's hat was whisked off his head in the increasing wind and it skipped along the street near a woman's ankles and then stopped and sat at the corner like an obedient pet awaiting its master. A butterfly flew by my cheek and rose into a sky muscled with clouds.

We neared the wax museum and saw a small queue. James combed his hair with his fingers and took my arm. He paid our admissions and we entered. It was enormous, a Grand Hall with Napoleon and Queen Victoria in beautiful clothes. Their figures startled me, emerging from the relative darkness quickly like Mabel or even Hera, my lovely owl. Their expressions were life-like but frozen, stopped in one moment forever. I wanted to touch them, make them move their limbs, greet me. Their likenesses were equally surprising and comforting. I half relished being "fooled" by them as though it were a child's game. Living forever, wan and pale and thick-skinned and held in time, a memory. But still, the resemblances were uncanny.

James halted by the Sleeping Beauty he had discussed, a young woman draped upon a chaise, her legs crossed beneath her pink and blue gown. Waiting to be reborn. Her blue slippers hung barely on her feet. She was sleeping with her elbow across half of her face. Waiting for her life to be given back to her. To continue. I wished to see her eyelids flutter, but, of course, I did not. James was transfixed, wanting to go past the boundary ropes, a uniformed guard watching him.

"Do you think of Martin, your fiancé, often still?" He asked, his eyes on Sleeping Beauty, his ideal woman.

"Yes." I was not lying, exactly.

"Do you wonder what has become of him?"

"No, I was not terribly impressed with the seance." Which was not precisely true either. We began strolling through the numerous exhibits, the darkness clustered around us and then we came upon the wax figures doused with light from delicately placed lamps. "What do you think connects us to another human being?" I asked, still on the topic of seances and spirits.

"Empathy. Perhaps more than that." He looked back, at Sleeping Beauty. "An attraction of some sort. Two separate bodies or laws of physics. Either it is there or it is not."

We were before a figure of Benjamin Franklin, the American with a kite pinned to the top of the exhibit space. We were to furnish our own lightning within our own minds. Something left to our imaginations. I could not decide what real electricity would do to his waxen arm, or his actual one, for that matter. His bespectacled face seemed kind and patient. "Is it something not translated by the wax? Or is it a facial expression, a touch, the right word at the right moment?"

"I suppose we can connect to any instant of beauty, whatever that is to each person. And sometimes it is enough."

"We all have feelings in common—being human—even if they are different—life, death, entropy. We all share those."

James led me to an area hidden near the back that, when we neared it, resembled a wounded soldier upon a table and a nurse tending to him. I noticed that the soldier's dark cap had a brim and a gold band, and that the once-blue jacket had faded to a lung-coloured brown. The man was upon his back on the table; a whitish blanket covered him. His boots stuck out, over the edge. I knew him. It was a Crimean soldier. It was Martin, and it was the veteran at St. Thomas's Hospital as well. It was all the soldiers we saw and tended to. He had an ashen face and an overgrown beard and mustache. But he did not move or moan or make any sound. It was what was above him that shocked me most and I almost cried out. It was Flo carrying a lamp. I could not believe my eyes. She was unchanged from eleven years ago. I nearly ran into the exhibit to touch her face, wet her cheeks with happy kisses. I was surprised to see her.

"Flo?" I said although I knew she would not and could not answer.

James laughed a bit and held me back by my arms, as I had been compelled to do with him and Sleeping Beauty.

She wore a simple yellow dress, buttoned down the front and a long, flowing skirt that would have been impractical at the Barracks, that would have swept up all the grime and filth. Her hair was knotted into a nest at the back of her head. Her visage was steely and concerned for her waxen patient, who could not die.

"But she is not dead, is she?" I whispered to James.

"Not all the figures are of the famous deceased. Some are still very much alive, Pain." He led me outside.

I took deep breaths of the gray sky outside, still thinking of the gray figures inside. The horizon was a whitish gray against a deeper gray. There was too much lifelessness in the air and all around me. I realized how much I missed Flo from almost seeing her. I leaned against the blonde blur of James and took more breaths. He was tending to me, which had always been my work with others. I had wanted to hold Flo, shake her into life. I understood now how he felt about Sleeping Beauty. It was such a shock.

I do not remember us returning to the house but we did. James said that I attempted to break away from him on the street, wander off somewhere. I found myself upon a chair where I read poetry most of the afternoon under the eyes of the household. Wordsworth and Coleridge. Kubla Khan and the stately pleasure-dome. Rime of the Ancient Mariner— about losing what is precious to us. What about losing what I did not have to begin with? My head rested upon my books. I wanted to sleep but could not. Finally when the remaining watery sun disappeared and I was no longer being watched I surreptitiously grabbed my cloak and hurried outside unseen. I began creeping along house walls in dark, dirty alleyways. I heard screeching and vaguely remembered thin, small bones pressed into my palms. I next discovered a strangled stray cat at my feet and gray fur lining my fingers. I brushed off my hands. Had I been sleepwalking? Its tongue lolled from its mouth and its eyes were open as it lay on its side. An old beggar started down the alley toward me, then stared at me, kept his eyes upon mine as he retreated, walking backwards, his rags flapping, into the cobblestone street.

I sauntered home and slipped back into my bedchamber and picked up a travel book about Africa but I could not read it, the words swirling too much. I closed the drapes in Rose's room and prepared a dose of laudanum for myself. First I wanted to write to Flo.

*My Dearest,*

*I saw your likeness today at Madame Tussaud's Wax Museum. You have become so renowned since the Crimean War and I feared you had died since I saw you last—over ten years ago. But we are both alive and struggling with our separate lives. I went with James, who has become a good companion. Especially when I desired to run up to your wax imitation and help with the patient.*

*Speaking of which, there is a veteran at the hospital who has been solicitous to me. We have not had much chance to speak yet of the war but I hope that we will. He appears to be quite decent and understanding.*

*That owlish woman from the hospital, Mabel, the one with claw-like hands, has been taken on as a project by a lovely woman whose friend died suddenly and recently. I hope it will work out to everyone's benefit.*

*I was thinking about that night in August, 1855 when that beautiful town, Kadikoi, burnt down completely. Two hundred houses as well as women and children all aflame. It began at one in the morning and finished by five. Remember? Only four hours for so much destruction. There was no wind, only a full moon that night that rested brightly upon the blue water of the Bosphorus like a giant eye, witnessing it all, cold and white. The fire had spread in that stillness until Kadikoi was a large, red blanket across the sky. The silence was terrible. It was pierced by a dog howling occasionally and the cracking of spent wood. Remember, we were awakened and told the Barracks were on fire. But we saw it was not so. It was quiet at Scutari with men wandering out, smoking pipes. So we walked out and spotted Kadikoi. The orange blaze followed one long line out toward the sea and only stopped at the water. The red, bursting pinwheels of smoke were almost a mile high. It was as though we were trying to extinguish the sun for the next morning. It seemed impossible. Until, finally, there were no more wooden houses or people to burn. It reminded me of a heart that has been burnt and is done with everything all around it.*

*Yours*

## The Art of Attraction

Surrey Gardens, the temporary home of St. Thomas's Hospital, was in full bloom. The arched windows peered upon all manner of yellow jonquils, purple hyacinths, the long, great arms of trees bursting with pink and white flowers. All was in a frenzy of colourful display. This was the art of lovely flowers, from nothing but sticks and stems. Bushes pressed themselves outwards and climbed past my knees as I walked by. All was expanding and turning inside out, pushing to show its inward beauty made outward. And a variety of fragrances covered the slight tinge of horse refuse, the sewers, and the smell of wet grass. I could hear water splashing from the scattered fountains. It was said about St. Thomas's that "you were not the same person leaving as you were entering." But that was also true of both the Crimean War and the dressmaker's. For we were continually changing—with luck for the better. Just like the gardens. And I understood the purpose of nature: that things must die in order for other things to live.

Inside the ward Jane was fussing with Carrot's blankets. Carrot made little gurgling noises and was likely sleeping or she was near to attaining sleep. Jane coughed raggedly and arranged beakers upon a tray. There were several new patients. The veteran sat up in bed reading a newspaper.

Dr. Lawrence went to the veteran's bed and sat upon it with

his legs over the side. His fingers tangled in his beard, his eyebrows grew nearer, "You will be leaving us today."

And the veteran nodded, holding the folded paper in his
damaged hand, his down-turned mouth unopened.

Dr. Lawrence left the veteran and I sat by him.

"You miss it, don't you?" the veteran said. "I mean the
war."

"Yes. How could you tell?" I crossed my arms.

"It's as if only a part of you is here now. Some part of you
is missing." He placed the paper on the ground and his hand
crawled along the bedsheets, resting at the top. "My name is
Richard Wellfield, by the way." He shook my hand and I felt it
was half empty, a space for his fingers.

"Miss Ann Russell." I shook his hand vigorously and his
hair bounced about his shoulders.

"I know. Do not worry, Miss Russell, there will be another
war."

"Not soon, I hope." I had not been reading the newspapers.

"It's that there is always another war."

"I suppose I do not miss it exactly. It is where I truly learned
nursing and had more purpose."

"You are purposeful here."

"What happened to you during the war?" I could see Jane's
tray banging to and fro and Dr. Lawrence conferring with a
new patient.

He told me how he lost part of his hand on the 28th of De-
cember 1854. The fingers were shattered by an exploding cache
of small-arms ammunition. A fatigue party and Richard were
placing nine tons of it in the chamber of a windmill close to
the First Division. The French aided them since their encamp-

ment was within 150 yards. Twenty men were at the mill and they carried the wounded toward the hospital when an English ambulance came and carried them the rest of the way. He was frostbitten and felt low and faint and the doctors thought about amputating the hand. But there were men there who were worse. They did not use chloroform and quickly removed the fingers and placed him in a trestle bed with three blankets underneath him and two covering him. He remembered one blanket had black stripes that looked like dark roads leading to nowhere. On the third day they placed him in a Malta car, a commissariat cart, which shook terribly and took him to a vessel in the harbour. They sat in the harbour for four days while more sick were loaded and then they finally left, arriving a mile from the Bosphorus. They docked there for several days until a steamer picked them up.

There had been no mattresses on board but each man received an extra blanket, and the worst-off patients, about twelve of them, had two extra blankets. All the men lay upon the deck, their heads along the sides of the vessel. They were packed close to one another with room only to turn. The air was foul, especially at night, owing to diarrhoea and the proximity of bodies. The convalescents and orderlies assisted the men with utensils fairly well and the doctors attended to all the cases. They lost 22 men out of 220 and two were wounded.

There was no want of medicines or food and the men that were on full diet got ship's rations. The worst cases received port wine, sago, and seaman's dough. Richard's hand was dressed every other day by the doctor. Sometimes the meals were late but the men did not become too rowdy or complain too much.

A military officer, Captain Samuel, of the 87th, was in

charge and checked upon complaints and made certain the orderlies completed their duties. Some men on board said that
the orderlies could be very bad indeed when the orderlies had
not been looked after with better food and extras. The orderlies
would ignore the men or make as if to push them off the ship.

When they landed they were taken to the Barrack Hospital,
my hospital, and he saw a doctor that evening. The doctor did
not dress his hand until the next morning and did not look at
it when Richard had first arrived. The doctor inquired as to his
health only. Richard lay upon a mattress on the Turkish divan
that circled the ward, as there were no bedsteads. He said it
was very dirty. He was given sheets, blankets, a pillow, and a
rug and was comfortable and received warm victuals. There
were several wounded on the ward and the rest were dysentery cases. He was given flannel drawers and shirts, and wine
every day. He felt he received kind and considerate care from
the doctors and nurses and had no complaints.

I thought of all the men we had lost to dysentery and all
the feet and hands lost to frostbite. I told him about the earth-
quake Wednesday, February 28th, 1855, for he was gone from
the hospital by then. How almost two hundred patients ran
into the Main Guard at Scutari and two leaped from the windows. Some that were out of their beds could not crawl back
into them again. Two minarets of Constantinople crumbled
and I believed the ancient towers on the barracks would fall.
All shook intensely and though my feet left the ground for only
a few moments, it seemed an eternity. Half of Brusa was in
rubbles with many people killed. A compound-fracture patient
was seriously hurt by scrambling from his bed. The shocks afterwards had all the patients worried again.

Then we talked about how lovely it was, viewing Sebasto-

pol. How I had mailed to my sister a Minie ball that I had discovered in the ground littered with shells and shot, an artillery
garden—one that I hoped would never bloom like the garden
at St. Thomas's. Yet the flowers persisted in Scutari also—with
a small, red Tormentilla, yellow Jessamine, and many low,
flowering shrubs the colours of vivid church windows. There
were bushes with ragged pink petals in the shapes of exotic
fruits. The remaining minarets and domes of Constantinople
rose looming behind them. The indigo blue, quiet, reflective
sea was filled with fleets, ours and the Sardinians, and the
glossy, kaleidoscopic hills.

"I can easily say that I do not miss the war—at this point,
any more than I miss my fingers." He wiggled his remaining
digits. "I am not quite like you."

"It is not the war I miss, of course. But the camaraderie and
the higher purpose." I thought of Flo in both these things.

"That can be found elsewhere." He handed me a card.
"Here is my name and address if you need anything, Miss Russell." His hair was coiling in the air like smoke.

Carrot began to wail again and Raphael's Madonna stared
at the child from across the room, her own silent baby in her
arms, her dress a red basin. Carrot's mouth snapped open and
closed, her wan eyes squeezing out tears. Drool spilled from
her mouth down her chin and onto her neck. Her weepy eyes
were intent upon Jane. Jane's chest heaved with coughing even
as she lifted Carrot, wrapping her tightly in her blanket. Carrot
stopped crying as Jane cushioned her in her arms.

"Did you kill many men?" It came out of my mouth unbid-
den. I covered my mouth with my hand but it was too late.

"Several. Most were younger than I. We had swords, bayo-
nets, muskets, hand-to-hand encounters, pistols, whatever was

handy, including a Minie rifle." And he smiled. "Their eyes were so filled with fear that I could only aim at their softer parts."

Jane called me to her. "Here, you take Carrot for a while. I need to fetch a patient's medicine." She handed me the bundle.

Carrot was sleeping, her crusty eyes tightly shut. I gazed at the Madonna and debated religion as a higher purpose and decided—yes, if it pushed a person toward their fulfillment, their reason to live. But it did not always do so. For Flo it did. For James it would not, science would. I was still undecided. I tried to place Carrot back into the borrowed cradle propped upon the bed but she began to fuss and whimper. So I walked about with her until she was soon asleep and then I slipped her back into her cradle. I wiped the dried spittle from her mouth and she sighed and tried to turn onto her side, her awkward fists hitting my handkerchief.

"Miss Russell." Dr. Lawrence emerged from a doorway, on his way toward another doorway at the end of the ward. His beard undulated against his neck as he spoke. "I forgot to give you this card from the woman friend of that patient that died of puerperal fever." He rummaged through his pockets and handed me a card with Elizabeth's name and address. "She asked for you to come by." He tapped his remaining pockets. "I have had a very busy morning."

"Yes, I know," I said. "Thank you, Dr. Lawrence." And I turned, grasping the card in my palm, feeling its hard, stiff edge creating another tense line in my palm. I slipped it into the deep pocket of my nurse's apron where it lay next to the veteran's calling card.

~

I knocked at Elizabeth's door earnestly and sternly. The door opened a crack and was then thrown wide apart. The hallway was plain but decent with narrow rugs and a table. "There ye are," Mabel exclaimed, "finally. She's crying in the bigger room."

"My, Mabel, you are looking well." Mabel wore a sky blue dress that fit her and women's brown boots laced up the front. Her hair was neat, nested in a bun. She had a touch of colour in her cheeks. Her sunken mouth was working.

"I ain't had a drink in a week." She held out one bony hand, which shook, an insect's wings hovering in the air. She grabbed that hand with her other hand, imprisoning it. "But she says it'll get better. Then I kin hold meat to me mouth."

"Is Elizabeth able to see me?"

Mabel showed me to a plain drawing room with a wooden floor, two coloured prints, heavy-limbed and squarish wooden tables, one floral rug, and several knobby chairs with inexpensive, faded, brown fabric. The overall effect was of a stew with chunks of mutton that had been boiled too long. Several vases with some bent flowers lay underneath the tables or behind chairs. One was broken into three large pieces and the flowers with scattered petals lay strewn on the floor soaking in small, shallow puddles of water. Elizabeth sat in a chair, her head in her hands, only her golden hair scampering, messily draped over the arms of the chair, cushioning it. She was sobbing. Her dress seemed buttoned incorrectly and slack, her stockings peeling and flapping over her shoes, her sleeves pushed up revealing her arms, and her fingers dug at her face. She was beginning to resemble Mabel.

"Mabel, you must go to the market for some meat, a cabbage," her blotchy face said.

I heard the door open and close. Elizabeth resumed her crying and I knelt, lay a hand upon her bare arm that seemed to tremble. Her lovely pointed chin jutted out from the heap of this sorrowful Elizabeth.

"It is Mabel," she sobbed, "I cannot bear her fits anymore. You see, she has broken so many vases I must hide them from her. She is too difficult."

"She appears much improved from your care." I gripped her arm, her soft skin in my palm. "Abandoning drink has made her boiled skin rosy." I half stood and she hugged me, her tresses separated into shimmering blonde strands that spidered my bosom and shoulders, clinging there and staying as she lay her head at my neck. Some of her hair stuck to my lips in a fine web; I chewed it slightly, tasting lemon.

I recognized her desperation as my own—with patients and family, the responsibility of care. I also glimpsed her loneliness and that Mabel was not much comfort. Elizabeth must have seen it in my eyes.

"It is not only her. I miss Rebecca Drake, my other friend, very much." She twisted her nose into the curve of my jaw.

I felt tears collecting along my clavicle and then at the back of my neck, cascading down my spine, probably staining the back of my dress. There was nothing I could do. It had been a mistake, Rebecca Drake. Perhaps Mabel also. Her hair whipped about us and I held her long back at the base of her spine. I detected a whiff of drink upon her breath. And then we were kissing and I was certain she had touched wine, as wine coated my mouth. It was a ragged and rumpled kiss as though we did not fit together and yet it went on for a long time. Her lips were cool and the kiss was a puzzle changing size, position, shape, trying to lock the disparate pieces together but we were unable to do so. I ran my unthinking hand along her naked arm and then along the edges of her neckline. Her hungry hand outlined my breast. And then the front door flung open and slammed and we fell apart. She wiped her reddened eyes. My mouth tasted of wine and lemon. I saw that she was still beautiful though she had not yet surfaced from her apparent sorrow. She flicked the errant hair from her cheeks and began to smile at me. My own blood roared, shimmied through my veins. I did not know what I wanted—what was before me or something else, something I was still waiting for, like God. Someone I believed could make sense of my life—if that was possible. Flo, for it was always Flo. I straightened my dress although there was no disorder in it. I could hear Elizabeth's breath, her exhalations, could feel them mingle with my own as we were still standing closely. I wanted to touch her cheek with my hand, to calm her further, but I did not. I had not seen any sign from her. I had still not had any sign from God as to my path. Any would do. I awaited the voice Flo had already heard three times, although perhaps Mrs. Tatterspol could have helped, even in the midst of my own doubt. She represented many voices.

Elizabeth seemed revived, even her window curtains fluttered with animation. She straightened her hair, her mouth curved into the shape of a new leaf. I felt as if I myself had drunk the wine washing my mouth. Mabel burst into the room and I could not catch her gaze. Her calf flashed from beneath her dress and I did not mean to see it. I could feel colour staining my cheeks.

"I got us a nice piece a meat, full a fat." She sat in a chair and pulled at the toe of her muddy boot.

"Very good, Mabel. I know you try to be good," Elizabeth said. "And you are." Her face was smooth and dry.

I noticed how her rug was worn, the paneled wood walls nicked. I focused upon a pair of white gloves strewn over the mantel, next to a plain, wooden clock, above a looking-glass marbled with dark veins. Several painted, porcelain figurines of dogs were positioned across the mantelpiece. One ear of a dachshund was chipped, though it was turned the other way so as to hide the blemish.

Mabel smiled, "I made short work of the gammon and eggs this morning, didn't I, Miss?"

"Yes, you most certainly did." And aside to me, "I need to work on her manners still."

I believed that I was more knowledgeable about the body than I was about the heart or mind, although I tried to understand both. And I missed the hospital, even Dr. Lawrence. The clockwork of the body being easier to understand than love or desire. I had known so little of either. I was distracted by my bitten fingernails, by the shadow of mud Mabel's boots left upon the threadbare rug when she took them off and wiggled her toes webbed with stockings. The afternoon sun was dwindling and the light that filtered through the flimsy curtains, framing all three of us women, was turning red. We were a dream I could turn to in the middle of the night. The air in the room was watery and thin and darkening. There was silence except for the quieting birds outside.

"I must see to my hair," Elizabeth said clutching a fistful of her yellow tresses as though they were wayward grass. She left the room, her mouth still upturned.

"How are you faring, Mabel?" I sat in a chair.

Her legs wobbled a bit when she stood, her wrist brushed

a tabletop when it flew from her body. "I'm learning to live with nary a drop a drink." She moved closer to me. "I know it sounds strange to ye, but sometimes I miss them rats. I named em all—Sam, he'd come up quickly on me, and Betts was always begging and there was Lily creeping about—acting like she'd seen it all. They wasn't any different than people." Her mouth was crusted with white. Some sort of liquid had bubbled and dried. "That there Betts was a fat, little thing."

"I miss my own owl, Hera. Some days I can still see the world through her eyes."

"Wot happened to her?"

"She died when my mother and sister forgot to feed her when I went away to the Crimean War." She was before me, shaking somewhat from lack of drink. "I had a fiancé there. His name was Martin Farland and he was a soldier who died in the Barracks Hospital there." I did not know why I told her firstly about my real life and then secondly about my untrue life. Neither mattered to Mabel. Perhaps it had been Elizabeth's kiss.

"I like you," Mabel said clutching my arm with her strong but unsteady one. I could feel the bones spread out in her hands like a rake but crushed thin in parts. Her eyes darted about the room, at the door. "I want to tell ye to beware a that one." She nodded at the door.

"Elizabeth?" I exclaimed, startled. Her savior.

"That one likes to watch me undress. She tried to kiss me yesterday but I turned away. I'm not sure what she'll have me do." Her beige stockinged feet twisted into one another and her arms crossed and twined. She was trying to become smaller, to move in toward herself, contorting a bit. Or else it was still her body missing the drink. I did not know whether to believe her or not. I did not know what to say. Mabel began rocking in her chair and it creaked as she did so. I stood up to leave and she seemed a hunk of bread that had risen funny and lopsided. She stared at the too thin rug as though it could defend her. From Elizabeth, or perhaps, from me. She seemed so alone and tiny and withered without her cellar, the hospital, and the rats. No capering here. In a sense, she was in Elizabeth's cellar with boundaries, no rats, and better food. She peered at me as I walked out the door, but I do not believe that she saw me blushing.

# The Ghost Illusion

The gauzy, gray morning dotted with new red and yellow blooms became a gauzy gray evening that felt thick and aqueous as though I were caught and held beneath lake water. A bright hem of last sunlight fell through the numerous clouds just before evening arrived with a large, scarred moon watching over us. The "us" included James, Mrs. Thompson, Mrs. Tatterspol, and the couple that had attended the previous seance and myself. Sensations flooded me but they were quiet currents that coursed below my surface in many different directions. I felt that I was waiting for some seed to take hold of me, drifting, to spread out its borders, to root within me. I did not really know what it would become. I would have to wait and see as the evening grew darker and darker. Finally, when the stars came out over the smoking chimneys and house roofs, and sparkled like jewelry laid out against black velvet, there was a knock at the door. We had all been waiting in front of the fireplace, sipping sherry and wine. I had been at the window searching through the faint, sprawled constellations for night to arrive. The moon stared back at me, wide and empty, a crushed white. Mrs. Tatterspol was calm and confident sitting by Mrs. Thompson, who was her usual peppery self. Both women wore black silk gowns; Mrs. Thompson's dress was high-necked with ruffles and Mrs. Tatterspol's was curved just above her bosom, which jutted out low upon her body. Mrs. Thompson wore a simple set of pearls while Mrs. Tatterspol resembled a jeweler's shop with layers of necklaces crisscrossing one another with black onyx, as well as some orange and purple stones, bracelets, and more than one ring on several of her fingers. The couple grew quiet as evening approached and they began to hold hands. James paced upon the rugs soundlessly, occasionally pulling out his pocket watch. His endless walking to and fro made the fire veer first one way and then the other as if a large storm were directing its position, hurtling through the windows, pushing it about. But it was merely James.

"When did you say your friend would arrive?" He stopped and whispered to me just before we heard the knock at the door.

"He said evening and it is only now getting dark." I sipped from my almost empty drinking-glass. I had invited Jean E. Robert-Houdin, a famous conjurer, who had visited the hospital to see a friend and concluded by entertaining patients there with his magic tricks. He also investigated mediums, but I had not told anyone that. He said he would happily do me this favor.

But when Mary showed Mr. Robert-Houdin into the room, she said, "Excuse me, Mrs. Thompson, but the strangest thing has happened—a bird has flown into the house through a window and is knocking about trying to get out. It's broken a flower vase." She bit her lower lip. "George, the gardener, is trying to catch it, Missus." She curtsied quickly and left. We could hear knocking against the walls outside the room, a shriek, the flapping of wings and then silence. I could hear Mary with a broom in her hands sweeping the walls and then as the commotion moved up the stairs, I hoped that the poor, innocent bird had not been caught in my bedchamber. All felt slow and poetic this evening except for James and the bird. I had said nothing about Mr. Robert-Houdin but that he was a recent friend interested in seances. We heard a man's voice at the top of the stairs.

"I think I have it cornered, Mary."

"It's very active for this time of the evening." Then there was a slam.

"There I got it."

"Bird stew tomorrow night."

I did not want to think about such a bird which otherwise could have been singing upon a budding tree branch tomorrow. Mr. Robert-Houdin walked toward me. With the window at my back I noticed a faint outline of the moon etched upon his extended forehead. As he grew closer the ghostly moon grew slightly larger. He lifted my hand and kissed it as the French are wont to do. He wore his evening attire that he said he usually wore upon the stage. James turned away and stood still, staring at the fire.

"This is Mr. Robert-Houdin. He shall be joining our seance."

"I am glad that you have arrived, Mr. Robert-Houdin," Mrs. Thompson declared, shifting upon the sofa. The sofa was a large, black, silk mass in the middle where the two women sat side by side and their skirts formed an enormous, black ocean.

"I am enchanted, Madame." He kissed her hand also and James swung around and glared at the new guest.

Just before we entered the dining room and were seated, I whispered to Mr. Robert-Houdin, "Did one of your birds escape from your jacket tonight?"

He laughed, showing several pointed teeth, dimples formed
at his cheeks. "Je suis non that kind of conjuror." His forehead
shone brightly with the candlelight. He laughed again. "No animals. Excepting my sons." He had a strong, square face that
I liked and trusted immediately. "Let us see what your Mrs.
Tatterspol will come up with."

"She is certainly not my Mrs. Tatterspol. But is a friend of
Mrs. Thompson, whom I stay with and care for."

In the room was a rectangular wooden cabinet that could
fit two people easily. A pale illumination glowed from within
and there was thin muslin across the front. The candle inside
swayed and then jumped, causing shadows to linger and then
race across the empty curtain. I felt a lively interest in the
night's proceedings, which I had not felt on other seance evenings. I was tired of seeing Mrs. Thompson conspiring with
Mrs. Tatterspol night after night. I doubted that Mrs. Tatterspol
could summon the dead—otherwise we would all be living
with them and consulting with them and they would be giving us advice even now. Yet some of these spiritualists were
excellent actors and actresses. I did not understand why some
people could not accept the limitations set forth by science but
tried to manipulate their way around them or through them. I
supposed it was the advent of the Industrial Age with its ma-
chinery and progress. And yet we were all bound by the laws
of nature, even if we had little regard for them. I, too, wanted to
immerse myself in the Other but I was more careful than Mrs.
Thompson. I, too, wanted the Truth.

I was seated next to Mr. Robert-Houdin and James. Mrs.
Tatterspol entered her cabinet "to achieve a further trance."
There were bells and the rustling, and the sharp sound of a
tambourine. I thought, "my, she is going too far tonight." We

could see that her outline collapsed and then revived through the filmy hessian. She was youthful and full of energy when she stepped from the cabinet. She sang part of a lullaby.

She drifted and nearly skipped over to me and said in a young girl's voice, "When will you be leaving my room?"

Mrs. Thompson gasped. "Rose, my darling Rose," she cried out and she fell to her knees, breaking the circle, which did not seem to matter.

Mrs. Tatterspol seemed child-like and her hair shone in the dim blue light, her eyes twinkled, her jewelry tumbled and scattered about her active body, polishing it. Then her body appeared to shimmer ghost-like, wavering, fading to and fro. She said, "I want to play there again with all my toys."

"I had not planned to return to my family until the close of summer. This was by Mrs. Thompson's request," I told her.

"What about me, Mummy? Have you already forgotten me? Are you tired of seeing me through the medium already, Mummy?"

"Of course not, my darling," she replied tearfully. "What should I do for you, my lovely child?"

"My medium would be closer to you and more comfortable if she were moved into my room." She giggled girlishly.

It did not sound like something Rose would be apt to say. But then it had been so long since I saw her last. I felt Mr. Robert-Houdin's restlessness and his eyes met mine.

Mrs. Thompson was about to speak. And I wondered what cruelty was. Was it cruel when a mother animal ate her young? Or a lion felled a deer? Was it worse to avoid the truth or meet it directly?

Mr. Robert-Houdin stood and took hold of Mrs. Tatterspol's sleeve and held it up, "Ah, but see this white powder. This is

the Ghost Illusion, is it not, Mrs. Tatterspol? That secret kept by
the Polytechnic people."

Mrs. Tatterspol disassembled, shattered like a vase into
many pieces. "I must go to the cabinet and give Mrs. Tatterspol the use of her body back." She ran to the cabinet where
her form slumped against the interior walls, her shadow curled
into itself. We could hear her mumbling about "certain harm."
Then she was silent and there was only her uneven breathing.

Mr. Robert-Houdin caused a bouquet of flowers to arise
suddenly in the middle of the table. "Did she use this trick
too?" We nodded our heads.

"She had only one flower materialize," the woman from
the couple declared.

Bells rang and a rapping occurred underneath the table.
"This too?"

We nodded our heads again. Mrs. Thompson piped up,
"But I have been talking to my deceased husband about important matters through her."

"My dear, you have been merely talking to your Mrs. Tatterspol. All these things can be explained by the laws of nature."

"But Monsieur Robert-Houdin, I have sold all my property
in Ireland as Mr. Thompson desired, all because Mrs. Tatterspol said to do so. And we also discussed what to do with this
house as well as other investments." Mrs. Thompson looked at
me and back at Mr. Robert-Houdin. "Oh dear," she exclaimed.

Mrs. Tatterspol's figure remained stationary behind the
unmoving curtain and I wondered how long it would have
taken a spirit to return Mrs. Tatterspol to her body. Mr. Robert-
Houdin strode over to the thin material and opened it saying,
"I am sorry, Mrs. Tatterspol, but I have made it my life's work to

expose the spiritualists. That is until I find the true thing."

But when Mrs. Tatterspol was revealed she was sunken into her copious jewelry. She was buried by it, unmoving and gleaming in the limited light. One half of her face, her right side, was melted as though it were waxen and hot and dripping. She slowly stirred one hand, her left one, and said with difficulty, "I cannot move my right side at all." Her raspy voice scratched at us.

I had Mary bring in more light so I could examine Mrs. Tatterspol. One rouged cheek was seesawed above the other; her features on her right side were slack and sliding off of her face. She could not move her right side at all and she had lost the use of all her muscles there. Science had again won over spirituality. I concluded that it had something to do with her heart.

~

When I knocked at Elizabeth's door and entered, Mabel, in a brown dress, said, "Tinkering with them bodies again today?" She held her raw, bony hands in the air.

"I could ask you the same thing."

Mabel ignored me and proceeded to a wooden table in the scullery where she was chopping up potatoes, onions, and a kind of lean, muscled meat that bled upon all the food, her hands, the knife, and the table.

"Do you think about the people in the hospital?" I had just left Jane tending to a young man with dysentery that she had hoped to marry when he was better. Dr. Lawrence said that he was not certain the patient would improve for he was so sick. When I told Jane what Dr. Lawrence had said she snapped, "Well, you are too old now to care about such things as marriage."

And, in more ways than she knew, she was right.

"No," Mabel said and I knew she felt no remorse. A woman needed to stay alive, she would think, in some form. It was the rats she missed most—they did not think about such things, they survived.

"What are you making for supper?"

"For the Miss. She can be a fussy one, ya know. She is someone who has not known hunger."

I could not say a word, never having known hunger myself, but Elizabeth was not terribly well off either. I watched the brooding sky in the window near her head; clouds were fanning out and then staggering together as though knitted by a Higher Source. Mabel's hands wobbled a bit holding the sour smelling meat but she was becoming steadier each day. She sliced off a piece of raw, pale-lobed, knotty meat and put it into her sunken mouth and sucked upon it. Evening, with its herd of stars, teemed beside her face.

"I hate it when things pretend to be alive and ain't," she said.

"Do you mean Elizabeth?" Or me? I wondered.

"Why, Missy? Interested, are ye?" She smiled, danced about the table, lifted her skirt to her calves. "Like a bit a this, eh?"

"Oh, Mabel. Where is Elizabeth?"

"She's a pretty one, she is. But I heard her crying last night again into her pillow." She danced again with the bloody knife in her hand. "She's trying hard to get me a job somewhere, that one is. Then I don have to stay here any longer. If I don find one I'm afraid a the kind a bawdy-house that one knows about, that she'd put me into."

"It is very nice here, is it not, Mabel?"

"I'm a prisoner here." She looked at me. "Until she figures out what she thinks I'm 'suitable' for." She put on airs in imitation of Elizabeth.

"Better than the hospital cellar." I was trying to convince myself as well. I did not want to become Mabel.

"Yes. But there you'd know when something was dead and gone."

I heard a carriage clatter by outside. The scarred wood of the kitchen table was bewildered and surprised when Mabel stuck her red knife into its center.

"Let Elizabeth know that I came by, Mabel."

"I will." She continued to prepare their supper, cutting up more small pools of meat.

"What kind of meat is that?"

"That be rat, it is," she said. "I found it. But don't go and tell the Miss."

~

I thought about kissing as I entered the ward. It was all about touching, two lips together briefly, a nurse touching a patient, the momentary afternoon sun causing new flowers to swoon. Two glasses of laudanum sat upon a table by Jane. They sat so close to one another that drops from the side of one glass had spilled and rolled down the side of the glass next to it. I brushed my finger upward catching the liquid and licked it from my fingertip as I walked by. A fly buzzed at the edge of the table, waiting for a chance at the laudanum.

Dr. Lawrence was busy at the table, his beard dipping perilously close to the place he was hacking and then suturing. When I saw the soothed, sleeping face of the man, I recognized the veteran with his patch of red whiskers and his wild hair cut more neatly, his head turned to the side slightly, the small, white hill of his scar visible. His mouth was slack and dreaming and therefore not so sad. Richard Wellfield. "He was in yet another fight. This time he may well lose his knee."

The war still went on, I thought. Even though others have taken its place since then. It was the one I remembered. My war. Flo's war. The Bosphorus, a chloroform dream that skimmed the edges of my thoughts so I became dismissive and lonely.

"How is your patient?"

Jane was blotting the forehead of the man who had dysentery. He clutched the blankets propped around him. He was young and dark-haired. His hands were callused and his swollen appendages twittered like fat beetles upon the bedsheets.

"Spongy," she answered. "I keep on filling him with water."

"More water," he cried out as if he had overheard her.

"We'll have plenty of water in a fortnight when we're married," she cooed at him. She commenced her wiping. To me she said, "Carrot is gone. Dr. Lawrence took her to the orphanage."

"It does seem too terribly quiet." I briefly thought that I could "help" Carrot avoid her miserable life if I tracked her to the orphanage, but then, she did not ask for my help. Not yet anyway. And there were those who could not ask for help yet needed it.

"Miss Russell," Dr. Lawrence barked aloud, "you may assist me if you are done with your rounds."

I moved the clamp, hemostat, the sharp beaks of the scissors. I bandaged the veteran's leg and loosely folded the bedsheets over him. I made certain he would face the window where bursts of pink flowers from a tree might remind him of battlefield explosions. I could not tell him that he had entered my dreams, my dreams of Martin Farland, the ones where I killed him again and again. In the dream Richard Wellfield stood by, watched as I helped Martin, took notes. Afterwards he said, "But you have done too much."

I answered, "I have married his memory." This in my repeating dream.

As though she were viewing my thoughts, Jane sidled up to me and whispered, "I do not know if he will make it through the night. Now I know how you felt about Martin." Her skin was damp and her face flushed. She was wringing her useless hands. For it was often God's will alone.

I did understand not being able to see someone you loved, whether it was of your own choosing or not.

And I remembered being a child of a mere three or four years of age, standing at my bedchamber window, and watching the stables as my father led out my favorite horse, Edwin. It was summer and the white, weightless curtains billowed around my still tidy dress. Their touch was so light and ephemeral on my arms that I was not certain the material had grazed me at all. Edwin had recently gone lame and was quickly entering old age. My father stroked his haunches gently and I could see his tail swishing away flies. My father then held up a rifle and shot him in the head, blood splashing the ground behind the horse. Edwin's ears twitched as he collapsed and his legs clawed the air from the dusty ground. I was horrified and clutched at the curtains, threw them away from me. My father then tried again to shoot him through the heart. I briefly wondered if my kind father would do that to me. And then I could see Edwin's organs working through the gaping hole of his scraped flesh. The horse rested his head against the earth and died. And I'd thought: so that is the inside of a body and how it works. I realized that it meant so little.

My father rushed up the stairs to my room. When he understood that I'd been watching him at the window, he said, "I have taken him out of his misery. Do not be frightened or concerned, little Ann." And he held me tightly to him. I grabbed one of his large, bendable ears. I knew that I would miss Edwin terribly. He held me away from him and looked deeply into my eyes. "It is all for the best."

I laughed, then nodded my head, and told him in my own way that I understood. I wondered, to myself, about the afterlife of animals. And then about our own.

And then Elizabeth entered the ward and perfumed it with her jasmine scent. She glided in, her blonde hair tucked into her neck, a dress the colour of tar pleated about her, a red vein crawled through her cheek, vexing her fine, delicate skin. She saw me by the sleeping veteran and hurried over.

"He is still here?"

"No, he is here again after being discharged previously."

She was staring at the glasses of laudanum that Jane had not yet removed, as if she knew something more about them. "I have two tickets to a public reading to be given by Charles Dickens tomorrow evening and I wondered whether you would like to attend it with me? I am hoping that it will aid in my understanding of Mabel."

"Of course," I said. "Anything to help with the mystery of Mabel."

"And afterwards I have invited a hypnotist who will demonstrate his art. He claims that a surgeon can operate using hypnotism in the stead of chloroform."

"In the interest of nursing and science I am curious as to the outcome of his forthcoming demonstration."

"I will see you then." Elizabeth relinquished us on the ward, her skirt fanning on the way out, nearly knocking over a pitcher. She barely exited through the doorway. Even when she was gone her jasmine presence still filled the room.

~

Mary's hair was haloed by candlelight as she crossed the library, tidying up. It was pulled back but could not help its nature. She was humming a ditty and the fire crackled rhythmically with her. I heard the bones of her neck creak several times, unless it was mistakenly the phlegmatic fire. Following Mary's example, I took to shifting books around in the study. Except that I looked at them more carefully. I hesitated with Alice in Wonderland, opening it and gazing at the illustrations longingly as though I desired to be transported to the hollow of a tree, creating a charming house, or even a treetop holding aloft a large, smiling cat. The spirit of restlessness gripped us all. James stirred the flames with a poker, his forehead furrowing, then he ran his palm along the mantelshelf. The curtains were drawn against the dark with its constellations. I sat in a chair with a book in my hand that I had no intention of reading. Finally James turned around, his hair flying out broomlike. The velvet curtains stirred.

"How did you meet this fascinating Mr. Robert-Houdin?" He asked accusingly.

"I met him when he was visiting a friend at the hospital and he then began entertaining the patients." I turned the page of whatever book was in my hands and glanced at the illustrations and fine words. "I am sorry if he has thrown your mother off her course of inquiry."

"I would not be concerned about that." He walked in circles around my chair. "The truth is not often comforting, as we well know."

"Yes, I imagine you have learned that from your discoveries."

"We are having a difficult time harnessing the energy. Taming it to a wire or some sort of conductor."

"Your experiments sound lively."

"Yes, they are." He clasped his hands behind his back. "Lively." Mary sang quietly, wiping the dust from books onto her apron. The fire jostled against the grate. "But I have heard that you met Elizabeth Donell who had been Rebecca Drake's companion."

"I met her at the hospital when her companion passed away."

He frowned and stopped moving before me. The warming air was still and dusty. "She has a bad reputation, Pain."

I laughed. "Many people are said to."

"Watch yourself with her, Pain. I am warning you."

"What have you heard?"

But the fire crackled hot and Mary's hair appeared to be full of embers and I did not hear what he murmured—something about drink and certain inclinations at least depending upon the situation, and houses for entertainment. Nothing I did not already suspect. His voice faded away when I wanted a strong and loud voice. Which was fine since I was not one that liked warnings or the business of others, knowing so much of what passed for fact was simply rumors twice removed. I would rather learn through my own experience. James fiddled

with the sleeves of his waistcoat as though he were talking to
his buttons. He withdrew his watch from his vest, glanced at it,
then began to leave the room.

To the back of his swinging, blonde hair I said, "I need a
new nickname."

~

I thought again of Flo poised over a soldier at the museum,
her own waxy, serene face floating, my name upon her lips,
and my heart stuttered as I made my way up the Thompson
house stairs. And then I imagined her saying, "Do not come
to me again. I cannot gaze upon your face." My feet trod heavily upon the stairs and my hand confided all to the banister. I
wanted to pluck the stars that were visible from the window
at the landing, throw them further away, to make more room
for the darkness. But the eyes of Mrs. Thompson's father rested upon me from his painting, accusing me of sordid deeds. I
brushed past the large frame carved with twirling vines and,
wishing him good fortune in death, climbed toward my bedchamber, Rose's bedchamber. His eyes followed me feebly and
I hurried. I was growing weary of the dead and the not-quite
alive. They had their own opinions too.

When I passed Mrs. Thompson's bedchamber, I heard
voices. I stopped to listen. The door was opened to the width
of my head. Candles swept away the dark and I believed I
heard singing, a woman's voice. I poked my head deeper into
the room and I saw Mrs. Tatterspol's ravaged half face part-
ing the portion of her lips that worked and a song poured out.
Mrs. Thompson, in her bonnet, stared at her intently. Then a
slight wind from the hall blew the candle flames to one side,

resembling Mrs. Tatterspol's face. And they both looked at me, caught in the doorway. Mrs. Tatterspol raised her good hand as high as her neck and bracelets clattered at her wrists. Mrs. Thompson came to the door in her stockinged feet and closed it. Mrs. Tatterspol resumed her singing, inside the closed door, and I turned and entered my own bedchamber.

I was weary of hiding so much about myself and weary of the lies we each spun to placate ourselves. I did not mind the killing any more than the healing. For was not love so close to hate? And what were the consequences? I had seen none. I thought about reading my travel books again. Perhaps about America this time. Instead I dragged out my wooden medicine chest and pushed aside the citric acid, essence of ginger, and carbonate of zinc until I found and mixed up laudanum. I supposed that people returned to what they believed or hoped no matter what the circumstances or truth of the matter. With some people truth or science was a waste of time. They had already made up their minds. The opium coiled like red smoke through the clear fluid. I mixed it and drank it quickly. As I lay in bed I pictured a lovely countryside with a plateau surrounded by full trees and shrubs heavy with hyacinth, rocks sporting sparrows, the sun gesturing at the rich ground. And then I peeled the landscape away as though the scene were a page from a book and behind it was a continuing war with cannons bellowing and limbs strewn across the green grass. Men yelled for assistance as soldiers tramped by. The noise was deafening now, compared to the country landscape where all that was heard was the twittering of birds or a warm wind stirring the tree branches. I could not return to my original image. I could not turn the page back although I tried. I placed my hands over my ears and snuggled beneath the covers, being tired. Faintly I heard a thump and then whimpering next door.

*My Dearest,*

*I have not heard from you for quite some time. Yet you are constantly in my thoughts. Please let me know yours.*

*Do you know much about magic and illusion and tricking the body into believing you see what is not there?*

*Yours*

## Kissing

Mary greeted me at the stairs when I came down for breakfast. Shadows from the gray sky in the window curled about the S-shaped legs of the dining room table as if they could hide behind the solid wood. James had gone after eating and the dishes lay scattered still upon the table in front of his chair. Nothing else was set for a meal. The dining room appeared ambushed and abandoned. Mary's eyes had deep circles around them and she was agitated.

"Now it's Mrs. Thompson who is unwell. The doctor came last night and Mr. James spent until this morning with her." She wrung her hands, not knowing what else to do with them.

"Why did you not wake me up to tend to her?"

"We tried, Miss Russell. But you wouldn't waken. You had your hands clapped about your ears tightly and didn't stir. We despaired and called for the doctor."

"I must go see her." But she placed a hand upon my arm.

"She's sleeping right now, Miss, and said not to disturb her till evening. The doctor said she had a fright and will get better with rest."

"What happened while I slept?"

"I'm not certain, Miss. Something queer with Mrs. Tatterspol, who was even worse for the wear."

"Where is James?"

"He has gone to his experiments, Miss, and will see to his mother later. He said that you should do the same." She curtsied and left and fetched me a plate of cold fish and bread. "I'm sorry, Miss, this is all the cook has ready at the moment."

"It will suffice, with a cup of tea."

Mary hurriedly retrieved a pot of tea, rattling the lid while the steam escaped. I was quickly awake. The house was quiet, yet breathing softly, waiting. There were rests at Scutari, in between the fighting and the noise of weapon fire and the lull between the loads of wounded brought to the hospital. We were busy between, men died, yet there was a calm in anticipation of what was yet to come. And it most certainly did come again and again.

~

I meandered through the hospital gardens, already late for my shift, yet I wanted to savor the colourful roses and chrysanthemums, allowing their showy fragrances and blossoms to remind me of the heaviness of passion, how it weighed upon a person, making them unfit to make decisions. I was free of much of that. Being a spinster, a nurse happy in her work, a woman trying to find her conscience in God. I watched others twisted by their emotions, resembling these rhododendrons falling onto their branches in their fullness. I thought for a moment of the Crimean soldiers who had too much drink and fell over their horses or into ditches. This day it was the sun's brazen influence as I swiveled my head into its warming glare. I once had seen a baby born with two heads; one much smaller—how it had been too much, excessive. It had died soon after birth.

In the window outside the hospital I saw my reflection, a
long, melancholy face with a scoff of dark hair and eyes that
hammered the glass. A sensible looking woman, but not a
beauty. I was not Elizabeth. Birds sang from the trees in their
enthusiastic, morning way—as if to the affronting flowers—
saying that they missed the petal's indulgence during the cool,
dark night.

Inside the ward I went to the apothecary cabinet and
checked the opium stored there. It was plentiful. The frail
odour of lavender about my person, apparent now, had been
no match for the Surrey flowers earlier. The colours of the liq-
uids and powders behind the glass intensified in the glittering
light, blistering the door and wall with streaks of red, orange,
green, and blue. I peered through the cabinet glass at the patients, at Dr. Lawrence and Jane distributing medicine and advice. I wondered if a conjurer could have healed them faster,
could bring the dead back to life. But, I supposed, if he could
have, he would have done so already.

I stood, brushed off my apron, and when I entered the ward
the first person I saw was Mrs. Tatterspol. Both rouged cheeks
were melting down her face as she had lost the use of both
sides of her body now. Her ample figure created large lumps in
the bed. Her jewelry lay quiet and undisturbed, dangling from
her ears, at her wrists, on her fingers, along her throat. None
of it matched. No one had bothered to take any of it. Her eyes
were closed and her hands neatly folded.

"That one is barely breathing," Jane said. "I arranged her
hands."

"You did well. She appears peaceful," I said. "I have met
her before at the friend of my family's house."

"She came in very early this morning in the state that you

see her now." She patted Mrs. Tatterspol's pillow and she did not move. "I don't think she'll be long in this world."

"I hope she will find comfort in the next one." I wondered. Or would she merely find more tricks there? What had killed Mrs. Tatterspol and sent Mrs. Thompson into her own dissolute state?

I quickly looked about the ward. "How is your man with dysentery?"

"He's gone," she turned away. "He died that very night you saw him."

"I am sorry, Jane. I knew you had plans together."

"It seems they were flimsy plans," she replied. "Not unlike you and Martin. So you know how it is."

I had lied again about Martin. Perhaps I did not know how it was to have someone you loved die. To see all your plans dispersed. Except possibly my father or Hera. Only someone out of reach.

Jane left to tend to a mottled, older man with his bedclothes rumpled about him. He was showing her his ankle swaddled in white lint stained with a brilliant red. I heard Dr. Lawrence's feet echoing in the corridor. Jane straightened her scarf-pin and her white cap.

"Hello, Jane," he bellowed when he entered the ward. He smiled and tugged at his beard while peering at Jane's patient.

"Hello, Dr. Lawrence. Seen enough duffers, prigs, and louts for one day?" She smiled and placed her hand in a familiar manner upon his shoulder.

"Enough for many a day." He smiled at her.

I searched for the veteran and found him in bed beneath the engraving of Raphael's Madonna; her eyes were fixed to the top of his sandy head as if he meant more to her than the child she held against her red dress, whom she did not seem to notice. He was scratching his reddish whiskers with his three-fingered hand.

"I have returned without glory." He seemed to have recovered his spirits as he sat straight up.

"And almost without your knee." I inspected it and it was beginning to heal.

"The streets can be murderous out there."

"So can taverns, dogs, and people."

"I cannot argue with that," he said. "I suppose I was foolish."

"As are we all. It merely depends upon the subject," I said. "For example, if a spiritualist dies does it mean that science has been justified? Or perhaps the spirits feel her work is done and they are calling her back."

"It could simply be God's work." He shrugged his shoulders.

"There are so many ways to see events. And all the chanced upon inventions."

"They are a sign of our times." I thought about trying a church in another part of the city, then asking God to give me signs as to what He meant. How did Mrs. Tatterspol fit into His plans? And how did I also? Elizabeth and Flo? Yet it all required explanation, which was elusive.

"When may I leave here?"

"So you may injure your other leg or some other part of your body entirely?"

"Precisely." His sad mouth curled as if he had been tickled. "I have received only kindness here. Perhaps that is why I like returning."

"And then leaving again?"

"Precisely." He paused. "Perhaps it is because of you."

"I do not think so, Richard Wellfield." I stood. The sky at the window was a cloudy metal gray. Jane's handkerchief fluttered to the floor at her feet. Dr. Lawrence ran by with a basin in his hands and did not notice the dropped handkerchief; he nearly stepped upon it. The fluid within his basin sloshed to and fro. Jane picked up her handkerchief, sighing, brushed it off, and proceeded to mop Mrs. Tatterspol's forehead with it.

I felt Hera's presence sweep through the ward—with her taloned feet, her large, white wings outspread, waving. I wanted to catch her and hold her this time. Press her beak to my cheek. My companion. I missed her conjuring my love like her prey. But she ignored me and flew toward the glassy window and disappeared. A medium's or magician's trick. The only difference being that a medium was solemn and reverent about his work while the other was not; the magician was playful and took it to be an illusion. An amusing one. It was then that I glanced at Mrs. Tatterspol and noticed her body slumped into itself, her head drooping. Her worthless jewelry lay quietly tucked against her white skin in a mound, glittering.

~

I returned to the Thompson house early, in the crocheted light of the afternoon, to determine whether Mrs. Thompson was feeling better. Tiny, pinkish petals flew, fizzing in the air before me, and then were swept into small heaps at the Thompson doorstep. Next the petals were whisked away, on the wind, to another house, to rest upon another doorstep. Soon I would be breathing the pieces of the tiny flowers. When I entered the house the smell of boiled cabbage, meat, and urine assailed me.

Mary and another housemaid rushed by with chamber pots. The odour reminded me of the hospital.

"How is Mrs. Thompson?" I asked Mary, who hesitated and scratched her calf with the toe of her shoe, balancing a chamber pot in her hands. The hall was suddenly cavernous and my voice echoed, up the stairs and around and about the large room. I was certainly not in the hospital. The ornate furniture shrank from our voices.

"She is improving, Miss. She asked that you look in on her." Mary squinted and left.

I went slowly up the stairs, stared unblinking into the face of an early Thompson ancestor and proceeded to Mrs. Thompson's bedchamber, where the door was characteristically ajar. I spied Mrs. Thompson in a bonnet and nightclothes stamping her feet heavily and then dancing about the room, her arms extended as though she had an unseen partner. She did not appear to be unhappy or hurt. Fu, the little Chinese dog, lay upon her bed, sleeping with his small, delicate head resting upon his outstretched paws. He sighed and turned onto his side. I knocked and the dog leaped quickly from the bed and stood before me barking.

"Shush," Mrs. Thompson said, gently placing the dog back onto the bed. "Come in," and she climbed into her bed, smoothing the covers over her. "Oh, it is you, Ann." She patted her bed. And I sat upon an indentation.

"I have something terrible to tell you," I said slowly.

"If it is that Mrs. Tatterspol is dead, I already know. She was in such a poor condition when she was removed." She petted the long hair upon the dog, straightening it. "And she has already come and visited me to say goodbye."

"Are you saying that she crept from the hospital before she

was gone?"

"No, silly Ann." She chuckled, rearranging the limbs of the dog. "It is that I, too, have a gift for contacting the spirits, to receive certain messages. Mrs. Tatterspol was helping me to develop them, when..." She froze.

"When, what happened, Mrs. Thompson?"

She stared at her hands upon the dog, at the candle flames married to the air. "She felt I was quite receptive to messages from loved ones—certain loved ones. I could not hear anything from the late Mr. Thompson but rather from spirits I did not know myself. Mrs. Tatterspol was uncomfortable as she was unable to do much with half of her body, so she encouraged me to receive the spirits that she could not receive any longer." She moved one hand in circles on the dog's back and Fu began snoring softly. "It was one thing I could do besides running this house and all the other financial matters."

I thought of the little she had done day to day and did not dispute her. "What happened last night?"

"When I do receive a spirit I feel tingling and my mind drifts elsewhere. Last night I lit some candles and after some time a spirit came to me, a man from Mrs. Tatterspol's past. All I knew was that it was not Mr. Tatterspol. She called him 'Harry' and inquired how he had found her since she did not want to be found by him. An argument ensued. I do not remember what it concerned. But then Harry slapped her and she fell to the ground and was in the state in which you saw her at the hospital. I do not know how they could have argued as Mrs. Tatterspol had trouble with her words but they appeared to have had a squalid fight. When I awoke I was in a fright. Mrs. Tatterspol was nearly dead upon the floor and my own hand was stinging. All I remember was Mrs. Tatterspol saying that she did not want to continue living half of a life. Harry said that her time in this world was waning and that she would be accepted with love in the next world." She pulled her covers to her neck. "No one in this house is to repeat anything I have told them. You shall not, shall you? I told the doctor that she fell suddenly. For there are many unbelievers, as you well know, Ann. I do not blame you for Mr. Robert-Houdin's rudeness, for he was not a believer. But you can see why I need a draught of laudanum to calm my nerves and to sleep tonight." The Chinese dog leaped from the bed and began barking at the wall, barking at nothing.

I left and prepared a drinking-glass with laudanum, the spreading red petals of calmness and delight. I thought about what she had asked of me, knowing full well that I have never conceived of revealing anything about someone that they would not want to reveal themselves. When I returned I said, "I will say nothing. Nothing at all."

~

I had nearly forgotten about Elizabeth and the Dickens reading. But I remembered late and donned a shimmering, flesh-coloured, silk gown that my mother had purchased for me just before I had left home for the Thompson house. It was a dress that described my body, extending it with a skirt, covering my neck and wrists. The slashes of lace, delicately placed, acknowledged that the material was not a part of my own skin. More the colour of the interior, the flesh of fruit. Elizabeth stopped by in a carriage that waited outside to take us to the reading. She entered and gleaned the spaciousness of the Thompson house, the heavy ache of the decorative furniture, the servants. Her lovely, shiny hair sat umbrellaed above her swiveling head, for she did not want to miss the movements of the maids nor miss seeing an expensive sculpture or painting. I knew she was impressed by the opulence of the Thompson house and that she wished for a better lifestyle. She lifted a heavy, gilt dish, as if guessing at its worth, and then relinquished it again upon the table. James descended the stairway as we were readying to leave. I introduced them.

"I have heard much about you, Elizabeth Donell," he said, his voice deep and strangling.

"Most of it kindly, I hope," she answered.

He gazed at her and then reached into the air as if to touch her near cheek but his hand froze and then returned to his side. "Yes, of course," and I could see he was enthralled by her beauty. Then he turned toward me, after fully absorbing her loveliness. "Miss Russell, I want to show you something in the library before you depart." James tussled with a handkerchief at his pocket. "Mother is well and sleeping, thanks to your ministrations." He looked up to the top of the stairs. "Excuse us for just a moment, Miss Donell." And he could not help looking at her again.

James pulled me hastily into the study. My face broke a small cobweb that had formed in the corner of a bookshelf and I peeled its threads off like a veil. The room smelled musty without a fire. He removed a volume from one of the shelves. It was a translation of the Grimm Brothers' fairytales from the German. When he opened it, fairies were flitting about the pages. He flipped to a story named "Sleeping Beauty in the Woods" that showed an illustration of a gold gilded chamber, a bed with opened curtains that revealed a young, beautiful princess asleep, her hair a long, yellow shawl covering her pillow, an arm tossed over one cheek. He ran his fingers over the picture and stared at it longingly.

"What do you think, Pain?"

"About what? It is a beautiful book and illustration."

"Do you not see it?" He turned the book right and left.

"What?" I could not help asking.

"Why, that Elizabeth Donell is the lovely girl in the illustration. She is the Sleeping Beauty."

"There is some resemblance, but Elizabeth is certainly not sleeping. She is downstairs waiting for me and I must leave for we are late." He was becoming obsessed with this mythical figure as he had once been with electromagnetism, and me.

I left James in the library with his illustration and hurried downstairs. Elizabeth and I dashed to the theatre. "It was a charming, large, and impressive house," she mentioned before we took our seats. Elizabeth pulled her gray gloves toward her elbows, her frog-coloured dress spreading between our seats. Her hand drooped over her seat, brushing mine, her small feet shivered in her shoes. I pretended to be a horse with blinkers, focused upon the reading, although thoughts of Mrs. Thompson and Mrs. Tatterspol scattered throughout my mind. Charles Dickens was an older man in his fifties, with darkish hair and a moustache that circled about his mouth and merged with his beard. He wore a bow tie and jacket and seemed exhausted from all his readings. He began:

"London. Michaelmas term lately over, and the Lord Chancellor sitting in Lincoln's Inn Hall. Implacable November weather. As much mud in the streets as if the waters had but newly retired from the face of the earth, and it would not be wonderful to meet a Megalosaurus, forty feet long or so, waddling like an elephantine lizard up Holborn Hill. Smoke lowering down from chimney-pots, making a soft black drizzle, with flakes of soot in it as big as full-grown snowflakes—gone into mourning, one might imagine, for the death of the sun."

And I imagined Mrs. Thompson, unaware, bruising the fading face of Mrs. Tatterspol, in a heap upon the floor. Did she feel there was nothing more she could do for her? Elizabeth wrapped her little finger around my own gloved little finger, hidden beneath the river of our skirts.

Dickens picked up and held another book. "Two years ago my Ellen and I were returning from a holiday in Paris and there was a terrible railway accident. We were more fortunate than some of the other passengers..," he said and then he began reading:

"It was the best of times, it was the worst of times,
it was the age of wisdom, it was the age of foolishness,
it was the epoch of belief, it was the epoch of incredulity,
it was the season of Light, it was the season of Darkness..."

So much betrayal and alienation. Yet it did describe these times, as well as others—although all was not dark or light, good or bad, but shades of gray—just like Mrs. Thompson's act—for I could not know her intentions—I could not be certain she understood them herself. Mine, on the contrary, were required to be clear.

The audience seemed quite pleased with Charles Dickens, jostling one another, incessantly clapping. Just as Elizabeth and I were leaving, a woman in garish stripes hugged Elizabeth. She was an older woman with a large diamond ring upon her hand. Tendrils of hair escaped from her hairpiece. Her accent was the shimmer of the sun, a lovely, warm thing tasted upon one's tongue. It would not tear petals apart like the wind but make them whole, put them back together completely.

"I heard John and Maria are visiting you after the reading to explain hypnotism," she lilted.

"Yes, as well as phrenology," Elizabeth exclaimed. "We must hurry home to meet them."

In the carriage to Elizabeth's house we kissed slowly, without speaking. My heart could not contain itself, but knocked against my ribs as if trying to escape again and again. I became lost in her lips, my world expanding and contracting, a breath shared by two people. It was an adventurous kiss, unlike any other. Unlike the one I had stolen years ago from Flo, hasty and dry, a spit. The carriage wheels rotated harshly and noisily bumped down the street. Our curtains were closed and I did not know where we were. I did not care. Our gloved hands intertwined. Her warm lips sewed our bodies together. Then the carriage stopped, the horse stamped its feet and snorted. We had arrived. We broke our kiss and went to Elizabeth's flat. I found that I rather missed kissing, a touch other than in solace, like a spirit circling about the earth, waiting to return.

Mabel wore her sky-blue dress and overlarge, laced boots. Her hair was neat and prim as she opened the door for us. "Glad to see ya. That John and Maria are involved in untoward business already. Hyp-no-sis." She sounded out the syllables and then smacked her mouth as though she disapproved or was eating the air.

"I cannot stay." I retreated from the door. "It is too late and I must go to the hospital in the morning."

"Oh no," Elizabeth sighed. "But hypnosis is such a scientific achievement. Something you could dearly use in your hospital work." She turned to me and took my hand. "We must meet again soon."

"Yes, of course. Soon," I said but I knew I could not. I wanted to, but what did she know of me? How could I tell her? For all the needs were there, lined up and waiting.

Elizabeth went inside and Mabel whispered, "Now you don get to see me pretending that I go to sleep and do what they tell me." She winked at me.

But I hurried away. I found an empty, dark, damp street. I heard some low moaning and saw that a wretched young woman from a nearby bawdy house lay in a heap. She was drunk and bleeding against a wall, refuse at her feet.

I approached her.

"Look at how they left me," she wailed, a loud voice from a small person. Blood was dripping from a deep wound on her arm onto her brash pink skirt. She held out her arm. She slurred her words as she half rose from the rubble. Candlelight approached and sputtered at a high window with a thin curtain at the other end of the alley. And then it departed and all grew darker again. Her hair was in messy tendrils about her shoulders.

"I am a nurse."

She grew quiet. "Do you want to fix me then, dearie?" She puckered her foamy lips for a kiss. She began sliding down the wall even as she grabbed onto it.

I stopped her sliding and held her. Then I kissed her long and deeply, surprising her.

She wiped her mouth. Smiled. "Want some more? It'll cost you."

"Do you like your life?"

"No." Her face grimaced. "What do you think, dearie?" Her hands in back of her gripping the wall.

My hands flew around her neck and I turned my face away so I did not need to look at her. Soon I heard a small gasp issue forth from her throat. She fell into a small mound back upon the refuse, a gnawed meat bone rolled out from beneath her. A splash of blood from her wound had landed upon my turned cheek and I removed it with a handkerchief. It was dark and quiet then. I snipped a tiny lock of her greasy hair and placed it into my pocket. There was little change between one moment and the next one after a death, except for their lack of struggling. I welcomed the silence, the lifelessness. I tended to her wounded arm with a torn piece of her own bright skirt without viewing her face.

*My Dearest,*

*Your silence is overwhelming. Do you believe that the body reveals us? Often, though, it appears that what you see is not what there is. However, I am speaking of illusions again. The illusion of Mrs. Thompson or Mrs. Tatterspol—who they appear to be versus who they really are. But that applies to any body.*

*Hypnosis sounds like an interesting technique—it reaches down and reveals the hidden into view, as well as stopping pain and bad habits. Have you heard of it?*

And I tried again.

*My Dearest,*

*Often I feel that I am dead inside and simply want the world to resemble how I already feel. The outside becoming the same as the inside.*

*I have vowed not to write you again until I hear from you. May I visit you as an old friend?*

*Yours*

But I feared that I was rambling and screwed up the papers and threw them away. The intentions of stars approached outside my window and I wondered at their thoughts. They were compelled to shine, no matter what else they had originally wanted or had thought of to do.

Part III

## Continuing

When I entered the hospital the next morning I was rather relieved to see that the veteran, Richard Wellfield, was already discharged and gone. As I looked at his empty bed, Martin passed briefly through my thoughts. The Madonna in the engraving was gazing sadly upon nothing, the lives before her filled with suffering and pain like so many human legs and arms and torsos piled at Scutari after the operations. The Madonna held her quiet child and then one by one we all disappeared. Over time. *It is the way of things*, her eyes said. Or perhaps she missed Richard Wellfield's company.

I felt the force of electricity as I pulled my apron over my head; it clung to my dress with small shocks transferred from my body through my clothes. It warmed my skin underneath in streaks and I knew I was happy to befriend James again, happy also to be doing nursing work in a hospital again. I wondered just then if I had been made of iron, and electricity had passed between the two materials, would I have become an electromagnet?

Dr. Lawrence walked briskly through the ward, his fingers rubbing his beard, his eyes upon another doctor whose back disappeared through a doorway. "Miss Russell, might we have lunch together later?"

"Yes, Dr. Lawrence." Jane appeared with a green bottle but

did not seem to have heard us. She tipped back the head of an old woman and poured the liquid into her open mouth. The woman swallowed.

After the ward was cleaned and the medicines for the patients were distributed, I collected the amputation pillows, so many that they seemed to rub my legs like cats emerging from bushes. The same way that clouds nosed into the sky. I began preparing some poultices. I readied some linen with cabbage to sooth inflamed areas and help with the sores on patients who lay in their beds too long. Comfrey and Selfheal, from teas, were good for wounds. From the kitchen downstairs came the smell of boiling slink, tripe, and broxy, and occasionally some better smelling tea. I could always explore what was available there for poultices.

A young boy of seven lay in a bed, his wide-apart eyes beseeching me. I saw his bloody skull where a piece of bone jutted out like a shelf. I neared him and realized that there were two pieces of bone resting precariously against one another, a hinge and a door. His hair was matted and sticky around his wound and the iron smell of blood was the same for a child as it was for a soldier.

"What happened to you?" I asked his flickering eyes.

"Aw, I tried to pocket some money from a rich gentleman and he banged me on top a me head with his silver cane."

"He hit you hard."

"But I still got a shilling from his trouser pocket and I'll get better next time." He closed his eyes. I was not certain he would ever open them again.

Jane stood over an old man with white hair who could no longer see. He was newly blind and his arms reached up toward Jane and waved as if he were in the sea and drowning.

She was talking quietly to him and he focused upon her voice. I could smell his personal odour from the other side of the ward. I saw her slip his misshapen, thin, gold ring into her apron pocket. She was not nearly as skilled as the little boy, but then she need not be with the old man. The eyes of the Madonna followed me as I crossed the room. They followed me wherever I went.

"Sometimes the patients, especially the old ones, are so grateful to me that they give me their valuables," Jane whispered to me. But I did not believe her and she did not care.

There was illusion and reality, what we believed existed and what actually did. Who we decided we were. Some days reality, like blood, coursed throughout veins, built up, and had a need for release. It was all a matter of where and when.

"Look outside," someone said.

All the patients that could walk in the ward rose and went to the window. There was a woman sitting outside making an abundance of straw plait hats to sell to passers-by later on. The branch of a tree lurid with white blossoms covered her head from our view. The sky, filled with frayed clouds, looked down upon all of us.

"Ah, reminds me of my old village," one woman patient said.

Outside the woman's deft fingers picked up the straws, weaving them, pulling a new strip into the fervor of activity every few lengths. In the ward we all laughed watching two finches designing their nest in the tree dangling above the busy woman. Their nest was messy with twigs falling around and about, and bits of paper and leaves bulged out and flattened. The woman weaver did a better and neater job, and her fingers were very fast. We agreed that she could have made

thirty birds nests in one afternoon. But I did not miss my county town near Nottingham where everyone knew our family
and their business. London was thankfully anonymous.

At lunchtime Dr. Lawrence came into the ward and said,
"I want you to examine a patient in another ward, Miss Russell." I went with him. Jane was busy with the seven-year-old
lad. They were playing with cards he had brought. For lunch
we ran two streets from the hospital and went to a food stall. A
frightful steam gathered and dissipated into the air above the
stall. But we ate our potato pies and some stirabout quickly. At
least we were away from the hospital and its odours. I sipped at
some tea that tasted peculiar but I could not say why. When Dr.
Lawrence's mouth was no longer full he said, "I have invited
you to lunch to ask you to watch Jane and tell me all that she
does."

"Why? Do you suspect her of something?"

"No." He was flustered that I had inquired. He had not
thought so far ahead. "But there have been complaints."

"Complaints against the nurses?" If he would not tell me
what he knew, I was not inclined to tell him what I believed I
had seen.

"No. Not specifically." He finished his potato pie. "But do
watch her and let me know anything that occurs."

I did not answer him. I stood. "We will be late to the hospital." And we hastily returned.

In a nook of the hospital the Isolation Ward sat with its
four beds, no windows, a rudimentary table and chair, and
peeling striped wallpaper. The black stripes often hung down
like beads near the heads of the sleeping patients, who no longer cared. I often came to this ward to listen to the patients as
they slept. It quieted my thoughts to listen to their measured

breath. Two young men lay in beds, one had had a severe sore throat, fever, chills, malaise, a rash, perhaps pneumonia or meningitis. He lay with blankets piled high near his wet face. Jane had been bleeding him and he appeared weak and shivering. I continued the bleeding and would stop it later on that day. The other young man lay as though he were sleeping, and his breath was sometimes ragged. He had been choked in a dispute with a member of his family, we had heard, and had not recovered. He had maintained this terrible state for three weeks.

Neither man had visitors any longer and had not for a fortnight. I liked to visit both patients, inquire how they felt, although I never received an answer. I left and negotiated the stairs back to my own ward.

Back in the ward, Jane and I stood at the apothecary cabinet mixing our palettes, some bitter smelling and others sweet. Some were odourless. Reds became pink; some blues turned green, others coagulated into purple. Certain mixtures were lumpy, others smooth. She pulled out a slice of some buttered bread wrapped in paper from her apron and offered it to me. I could not discern whether she was suspicious or knew I had already eaten. I thanked her and declined to eat. She ate the bread in three gulps.

"I hate the food downstairs," she said, "and it reminds me of poultices and medicines." Then she reached into the lip of her pocket again and brought out a yellow-green apple speckled with orange. A little round leaf hung from the stalk as though it had been newly picked.

"But I would like a bite of that," I said.

Jane borrowed a surgeon's knife, wiped it with her apron, and cut several pieces. She pierced one and offered it to me

from the end of the blade. A moon with an arc of silver stars.
I pushed the slice into my mouth and savored the tart, juicy
treat.

"What about that Mabel," Jane asked between bites, "how
is she getting on with that friend of the poor, departed Rebecca
Drake?"

"I must go," I answered her and Jane shook her head know-
ingly. I thought of Elizabeth and how my work, my calling,
separated me from everyone.

For I did not like admitting doubts, only certainty in what
I did. And I felt a need boiling within me like learning how to
breathe again. An urge that seemed right.

I peered into the dead-house room for inspiration. Several
bodies lay about on tables, one or two upon the floor, and one
lay propped against a chair. I placed my candle at the edge of
a rough table in the long windowless room. It was quiet and
peaceful. I felt calm and at home among the bodies although I
breathed through a rag I had doused with lavender perfume.
I inspected their limbs, stiff with injuries, histories, the details
of their lives. A child of six, a young girl, with a torn leg, and
near her, a man with a blackened arm. The child wore a long,
blue dress with eyelets; her mottled skin was nearly translu-
cent. Too much was visible there, bone, blood, muscle, and the
organs tucked underneath the jagged, open skin. I wanted to
speak to them gently, carefully, about their lives, about what
had happened to them. I held the hard, curved fingers of the
little girl. But I dropped them when I heard the doorknob turning. A doctor I did not know soon rushed inside. The fresher
air careened about him.

"Am I disturbing you, Nurse?" he asked me, looking about
the bodies.

"No, Doctor, I was just leaving. I did not find whom I was looking for."

"That is most certainly good news."

And then I thought how I was like that little girl, climbing trees, and getting caught by a branch, the eyelets of her dress watching her every movement, her mother's yes telling her what to do and her no what not to do.

I had stopped counting bodies long ago. Why? I had a need that returned again and again, a strange, fleeting desire. The touch of a long-gone hand. It had made so many men happy. A hidden fire that rose hurly-burly through my limbs and enflamed my heart, my fingers. It was a part of me, of who I was, like a stolen snip of a lover's hair. A final answer, a final destination. I would not deny it.

Next I found myself in the Isolation Ward, where the one man had bled profusely. I did not stop it, but allowed him to weaken further, draining more blood. The other man was scarcely breathing and I did not like the sound of his breath. I heard footsteps nearing the door. I spun about quickly to remove the tubes and tidy up, straightening pillows, blankets, the soiled sheets as though the room was wrong, changed, and too disturbed. The black striped wallpaper bent toward one of the men's head, brushing my arms as I circled about his face, moving frantically. I pushed the softness down upon the terrible, ragged breathing until it stopped. I could hear the tapping of a nurse's shoes at the door and a woman's low voice repeating a prayer. I looked up at the patient I had just tended to and noticed the pillow pressed down upon his face, which I promptly removed and set under his head.

When Jane entered she said, "Oh my. That one's face is bluish and this other one is gone also, seems to have bled to death." And she made the sign of the cross about her forehead and shoulders. "There's no more we can do for them," and she left.

I thought of Martin, the face upon my table, unfrozen, smiling, nodding at me. I knew that both men would have asked for my help if they could have.

~

Before I continued to the Thompson house I stopped at another Catholic church. There was nowhere else to go that was as peaceful, certainly not the Thompson house or the hospital. A blue-eyed statue of the Virgin Mary cleaved to the wall, her arms twined at her chin in mid-air. Her eyes were half closed, in meditation or contentment, but I could not help thinking of Sleeping Beauty and that both women were waiting for men to begin their lives in one way or another. One was waxen and one was wooden. They were both legends and both were suddenly awakened. I wanted to awaken also. I took in the wooden pews and mosaic windows, the Bibles lined up like dark soldiers, and I began to pray. The implications of air seemed immense. The body was overwhelming. I pressed my hands together and repeated any psalms I knew. I remembered a line from a Gerard Manley Hopkins poem I had read somewhere: "My heart in hiding/ Stirred for a bird, —the achieve of, the mastery of the thing!" How he had loved what God had wrought. All that there was had issued forth from Him. I wanted to know His intentions for me. I did not want to be discovered. I did not want to stop. I was tiring of my false self. I watched the late afternoon light persist through the beautiful windows and fall in refracted puddles upon the walls. The red was blood pooling

underneath a patient, the green was Spring spreading all that
grew about us. For what was ugliness and what was beauty? I
closed my eyes tightly and composed my own poem:

"So breathless when I saw her smile,/ So rare and so green,/ I
could not help notice the perfect face,/ Above the rutted chin.
"For she had been asleep,/ And Sleep had left his mark,/ Soon
all her beauty returned full force,/ Until she began to talk."

I began to contemplate the elusive nature of people, plants,
and religion. So close and yet so far. I was yearning, and then
it happened.

It was a moment. I was flooded with an incredible and terrible feeling that was a form of light. It was like the headaches
that some patients described, a raw pain, a pulsing light that
brightened, that infected all about them with a throbbing glow.
I had been lifted up and time had stopped. I did not breathe. It
was a moment like no other moment of my life. All that happened was internal, as if a part of the inner workings of my
blood, bones, heart stomach, lungs. And all my questions had
begun to be answered without the answers being specific, as
if they were a part of my knowledge already, as though they
were previous feelings. Any former anger or frustration with
God melted away, and was no longer significant. He seemed
to say one word that rang throughout my being, "Continue."
I had heard it, without it being uttered. I had finally received
my "Call from God" and it echoed throughout me. I desperately wanted to share it with Flo, who would understand, but
I decided to wait until she contacted me. I was agitated and
yet content at the same time. When I became aware of my sur-
roundings, I saw that a darkness had entered the church and

candles were being lit. There was a complete silence except for
shoes tapping upon the stone floors. I breathed the cool, damp
air deep into my chest and it felt lovely. And I knew I was to
continue nursing, to do God's will, to end the needless suffering. I had listened. It was how I had felt after helping a patient
die but even more so. Colours were more vivid, the air itself
more lively.

The experience cemented my will, made me feel more righ-
teous. I was certainly listening to God, on the right path. Such
was my conscience. I noticed my weakened odour of lavender
from my hospital work again as though it had just returned
after an absence. I looked about. There were a few people, a wavering candlelight. It had felt as though a whole lifetime had
passed, held within one moment. But I had finally received my
guidance, which I had requested again and again. I had to be
still and truly listen. I rested my head upon my arms against
the pew in front of me and fell into a deep, short sleep. When
I awoke the face of a patient from the hospital was fixed in my
mind's eye. I wrapped my shawl about my shoulders and head
and knew what I had to do.

I walked to the hospital in the late after-hours, avoiding the
night watchman. A few orderlies were cleaning but no one else
was present. No kitchen staff, nurses, or doctors. On my ward,
most of the patients were asleep. I examined the boy. He had
developed a fever and was delirious already. I rested my hand
upon his brow and then removed it. I went to the old man and
held his ringless hand. His white, dirtied hair hung in front of
his sightless eyes, like drying laundry that had fallen from a
clothesline. I could have inquired about his "gift" to Jane but I
did not. I asked him instead how he felt.

"I'm useless now," he moaned. "I couldn't do much for my

wife and family before—but now that I'm blind I can't drive carriages as I was hired to do before. My wife and family have thrown me out and the only place that'll have me is the poorhouse. My only consolation is that I can't see it. I'll be vexed by every pickpocket and poor wretch until there's nothing left of me. Please, kind nurse, I'd rather die. Please, nurse, kill me." And he began crying. The tears oozed out of his eyes, the lenses cloudy and the colour of whitened sheets. "I don't feel well here either." He thumped at his chest, then wiped away his tears. "I'm old and it's time. Please help me, Nurse. I want to die now, if you are truly kind."

It was those words that I had heard many times before. And I had responded to them.

"I do not know, sir," I said smoothing down his white hair.

"Nurse, I've heard your voice before and know you to be kind and just and strong. I'm certain you can do this one thing for me. I'll be forever grateful for there's nothing left for me now." And he grabbed my hand from his head and squeezed it as more tears flowed from his blank eyes.

"It is something that cannot be undone once completed," I told him carefully.

"Yes, yes, thank God. Please, Nurse," and he clutched my hand into a ball. He whispered, "Please kill me."

He had thought about what he wanted and I knew I would help him. I had seen his face in my vision. He was beginning to cry and I did not want him to awaken the other patients. "I shall help you," I whispered to his loamy ear and he calmed down, clutched my hand.

"Thank you. God Bless you." He kissed my hand with his foul mouth.

I went to the apothecary cabinet and mixed a strong dose of laudanum and whispered to him, "Here it is." I tipped his head back and he drank. He settled into his bed, his hands calming, no longer coiling in the air, searching.

I could not watch their faces as they died, falling as they did into a sleepful repose or an agonized grimace, seeing something in the distance that I could not see. I had viewed the bodies carted away from the barracks, afterwards, their limbs and faces contorted. I had tried to end their suffering but felt responsible for their last few minutes upon this earth, and their frightful, everlasting poses. I briefly looked at this man I did not know and who had no name that I was aware of. I could not imagine what his life would have been like since I did not know him and his former life. Yet he was affixed upon my mind like Martin and all the others. But I also needed to forget them or else they should rise up into my thoughts again and again as the flames did in a good fire, forming hot, orange waves.

I cleaned the laudanum from the glass and left the hospital, still seeing no one, hidden well beneath my shawl. A piece of his dirty, white hair knotting my fingers, plunged in the pocket of my skirt.

~

I was in a calm and composed state when I arrived at the Thompson house from the hospital. The stars twitched beside the big body of the moon as though they were torn pieces that had scattered and were now trying to return to their source. When I turned the corner of one street, a couple, with their arms intertwined, suddenly appeared from an alley and I was startled for a moment but quickly settled back into the happiness of having recognized and heard my calling, the true voice of my God, of having finished my allotted deeds.

Mary opened the door and we walked into the parlour. Several vases held weightless flowers with their hectic new colours. I wanted to tell her how remarkable His Word was and how I was happy to be doing His work. I was not tired at all.

"I should look in on Mrs. Thompson."

"She's sleeping now, Miss. But she says she needs you tomorrow."

She left and I poked at the remains of a fire. As it became a deeper dark outside it became chilly and damp in the room. My bones ached like hard, cold rocks. I pulled my shawl close around my shoulders. And then James, dressed in a waistcoat, with his hair combed back, walked in. I was glad to see him and have someone to talk to. I could hear Mary yawning at the open door, her untamed hair scratched at the doorframe.

"I want to share a Godly experience I just had in a church." I was not used to discussing such a thing. I stuttered. "I heard His Word and it confirmed me in my nursing work. It surprised and delighted me." I touched his arm without thinking. I was no longer completely calm.

He patted my hand and absently removed it. "Good, good. I need to discuss another matter." He rubbed his hands together, and then sat down in a chair. "Your mother and sister have sent my mother a letter requesting that you go home soon. In a month or so. I do not know if this shall ruin your plans or your hospital work. But Mother says that that time would suit her very well as she is rapidly recovering from her fright and illnesses and feels she will be well enough by then."

I gasped a little, having almost forgotten about them,

my family. They paled terribly next to all my experiences. James sighed and Mary coughed and yawned again into the distance.

"Now, what is this about seeing God and spirit phenomena?"

"No, James." I did not want to treat him as a child and call him "Slim Jim" although I was sorely tempted. "I did not see anything and there were no spirits. I heard a great voice that went right through me."

"What did this voice say?"

"Simply one word. Continue. And I heard it distinctly."

"Did anyone else hear this voice?"

"No one else appeared to. There were not many people in the church. But I feel I have personal communication now and it is what I have sought after for so long."

"What do you believe He meant? Could it have been from your own mind and thoughts in the way seances are?"

"I am still interpreting what He meant and I do not know where it is from. Is not all literature a creation of the mind? How about the discovery of electricity and electromagnetism? I feel that the unseen, deeper mind governs us, guides our actions much of the time. Then there is emotion and the body. But the unseen mind is the most important."

"Nonsense. Thinking people are governed by their scientific and logical thoughts and try to make conscious decisions. As in nursing—you do what has been deemed best for the patient. That decision is arrived at because certain medicines have been tried before and been successful. It is science and proof. Experiments. That is precisely how I am laboring right now. Experiments with electromagnetism. To see when it works and when it does not."

"But these are all invisible properties. If we do not see it, does that mean it does not exist? What about the way we think and feel? We cannot see that."

He thought about this and said, "Yes. Such things may not exist and it is up to us to prove that they do."

"Is not the product, say, the attraction of two magnets, the twitch of electricity upon a dead frog's legs, the obvious existence of our minds or one spoken word, enough?"

"No, Pain, it is not. It must be proved."

"How, then, do you prove the existence of electricity or electromagnetism?"

"By moving a magnet in a coil of copper wire that I might create electricity, and the opposite is then true for electromagnetism."

"Are there not two metals naturally attracted to each other?"

"Of course. But I do not think you want to hear about our experiments just now and besides, I am sworn to secrecy." He yawned and stretched out his arms.

"You are right. It is time to go to sleep," I said. I would cling to my own beliefs as Mrs. Thompson and even James have done. We were all terribly stubborn in our needs in the end. For James was asking me who God was, really.

We all departed at once and I looked into Mrs. Thompson's partially opened door as I passed but all I could see was darkness tempered by moonlight and my own candlelight. I could hear her snoring and I could make out a white frill upon a bonnet. In my own bedchamber I sat upon the child's chair, Rose's, which was certainly too small for me.

I thought back to one summer day before my father had died. He had gathered a fistful of grass and queried me, "What becomes of us when we die, Ann?" He allowed the blades to then fall through his fingers. His back was against a tree on our estate, all of it his, if one could truly possess land and the living creatures upon it.

I remembered lying upon the picnic blanket, listening to the hum of insect life hidden within the grass. Some insects escaped, flying toward the unknown. Some burrowed deeper, underneath the roots of plants, not to be discovered again. Some went on their merry way, busy at their tasks, unaware of the enormous humans who governed their fate. I brushed several ants off the blanket that had been attempting to climb my boots. Then they marched down the length of my skirt until I stood and shook them off. The sunlight mottled my father through the tree branches and made him seem hazy, fading. The grass he had held was heaped into a pile at his side, useless, once living, unnecessary to him even if it were his own grass. And I knew then how quickly everything changed.

"I do not know, Father. All I know is that all this," and I spread my arms wide, "continues without us."

Now with father gone, I did miss him sorely. And he had asked me about death before he was ill—a year before he died, when my mother and sister were busy with a regimen of social events and left us both to ourselves and our own thoughts. My wonderful father who had taught me all I had learned and was asking me a question. One to which I could not respond. I did not know what he would have thought of what I heard. He was not at all spiritual and called religion "a hopeful investment in the future. All awe and incantation." He called the Bible "consummate storytelling." I remembered his inquisitive, lively face beneath the thick leaves, the twigs that fell onto our clothes, his wise smile. I had stacked the errant twigs upon the blanket, next to the comfortable silence that settled, between us.

Now I turned toward Rose's white walls and whispered to my father, "Science is good, it is progress, but it does not have all the answers." Although he could no longer hear me.

I wanted to write to Flo but would not. It had become a habit difficult to break. I missed summarizing the day. I lifted the fresh, clean bedsheets and wiggled between them. Tomorrow was my day off from the hospital and I would tend to Mrs. Thompson, perhaps visit Elizabeth and explain to her that I was too busy for any relationship except for friendship. I thought about the life I could have had according to society—married to James, living in this house and not needing to return to my family home. Or, married to a soldier, with children, with the war and nursing to share. But instead I chose a life I could not have imagined when I was young. I could not conceive of anything but nursing. My family still disdained me for it even though I nursed father and many relatives and friends. I would always be the spinster aunt. Almost married to a dead soldier. I could not envision what my life would soon become. I could never live in my family's house. *Continue*, I thought. Yes, I would. Continue. I thanked God for giving me the time of day, the encouragement. An answer to my prayers and mumblings and beseeching. Continue. And then I fell asleep.

~

"James has been too terribly busy for me," Mrs. Thompson said, her night bonnet's frill tipped to the side, a tree whose branches were blooming down only one side. "And I do not know what I will do without Mrs. Tatterspol."

The skin upon her arm was warm and firm to the touch,

her eyes appeared to be clear after her night's sleep, her mouth was dry and whitened, but that was normal for Mrs. Thompson. She lay still in her bed but I could see a movement forming in her and I believed she would rise soon. "What do you mean?"

"I need her to sensitize me to receive the spirits. Do you know that Mrs. Tatterspol visited again last night?"

"No, what did she say?"

"She did not say anything but she motioned to me with her hands to follow her." She threw her hands down upon her covers, waking the little Chinese dog. Fu stretched, his tongue licked his nose and mouth. Then he settled back down again, a coiling of hair and haunches. "But I did not follow her. I was afraid."

"And well you should be." I fussed with her covers without disturbing the convoluted dog. "Perhaps she was saying to follow her figuratively, not literally."

"You could be right, my dear." She scratched her forehead. "I shall take my medicine now. I am ready, Ann dear."

I fetched a glass of water from Mary and went to my bedchamber and opened my medicine chest and knocked the glass bottles about as if I were searching for something. I opened Mrs. Thompson's bedchamber door and offered her the glass of water.

"It is so clear today," she said drinking it down in several gulps.

"Yes, it is a new medicine. Good for reviving the spirit," I told her.

"I will find what I need to occupy myself. Do not worry, Ann dear." And she threw her head back upon her pillow, knocking her bonnet askew across her face. The little dog began barking wildly at the window. He ran to the floor, stood on his hind legs and pawed at the glass. Then he jumped upon the bed and ran about in circles over Mrs. Thompson's legs, stopping several times to pant. Then Fu ran about again in more frantic oblongs like a string pulled tighter and tighter, about to break.

"I will visit you later, Mrs. Thompson." I gazed out the window as I was leaving. There were two dogs outside; one had leaped upon the other's back, eclipsing all but a black snout and soft, brown eyes.

~

"Mabel is gone," Elizabeth said when she first opened her own door. "To where I do not know. She has taken her two dresses and all her shoes and vanished."

"Oh, dear," I said, suddenly in her small drawing room, my hand feeling for a chair. I sat down without looking at the seat. Elizabeth's skirt swished as she paced, twisting and twisting, sounding like birds beginning to take off into flight.

"I discovered her gone this morning."

"Perhaps we should search for her." I noticed a vase with flowers the colour of milk already sitting upon a table.

"Where? The public houses?" Elizabeth's blonde hair shone, refusing all darkness and shadow. Her forehead furrowed, a vein pulsed at her neck, a river rising from her skin. I watched it ticking there, and red washed from her neck up to her face. Her fingers twittered like sparrows. "No, no. Let her go. Let her make her own way in the world. I have tried to help her and I cannot do any more for her." She paused, turning to look at me. "She did not even give me a word of thanks."

"I am certain that she meant to. We just do not know what has become of her." I did not believe that we would find her. Mabel had escaped as she had hoped to do. I sighed into my chair as Elizabeth wore her rug down further.

"It has also come to my attention that you had been confined after your work in the Crimean War, Ann," she said in an ugly fashion. There was a moment of uneasy silence between us, and Elizabeth's face darkened.

"Briefly, by my family," was all I told her, not wanting to discuss it. Not wanting to think about that unpleasant time that was all nightmares in place of sleep and agitation at every tiny movement. "I was exhausted," I explained.

Elizabeth crossed her arms upon her chest and stood still a moment and peered at me, her brown eyes shining, her hair lovely and burnished by the low light. "Perhaps I would not have taken her in to begin with if I had understood that the source was so faulty."

She was saying that she would not have had anything to do with me or Mabel if she had known. I thought of that sad, gray place where my father would come to visit me, his head looming at me, floating toward me nicely. He had held me and told me that my sister and mother would not visit. They were too busy, he had said. It was a sanitary place. They did not know what to do with us, the patients and ragtags from good families who had seen too much of the war or had other problems. I was there for several months in 1857 when my father did not know what to do about my nerves and my sudden, rough crying. "It is not like you, Ann," he had said when I returned. "You have changed."

All they had recommended there was rest. And it had worked. I grew stronger than before.

I flew out her door. I, too, left her stewing in her cruelty, and, like Mabel, I planned never to return again. I did not look back at her lovely face. I did not plan to ever say another word to her.

# Travelling

At the hospital I sat by the young boy's bed. I held his feverish hand and wedged some pillows behind his neck to keep his head still. I hoped his fever would leave him soon. I carefully applied a cool, wet cloth to his forehead and neck. He mumbled some words, mostly sums or numbers, I thought. Perhaps he was tallying the income he anticipated or hoped to acquire someday. After a few moments I stared at a red geranium on a window shelf over his head. The delicate, small nubs of blossoms were beginning to push out suggestively past the green leaves that held them. As one thing died, another took its place. The plant had been dormant for a while and suddenly decided to bloom. It appeared to thrive from its lifeless, hollowed stalks, inspired by Spring. The first blooms were always the most brilliant, rampant, and beautiful. And appreciated.

I pulled my chair to the other side of his sick bed and looked again at the Madonna and child. Was she also a Sleeping Beauty? Or merely caught in her gesture with her child? No kiss or touch could awaken her although she saw everything, following all with her dark eyes. Unable to act, she watched, observing without comment. She declared no responsibility. The wide, red spaces of her dress grew larger and then smaller as I watched, pulsing, almost alive. Her expression appeared otherworldly. It calmed me as well as her contented child. For some odd reason I thought of Elizabeth and how her beauty blinded me to her other attributes. How her breathing alone could turn the room's attention upon her, take up all the space. She created an ache, a ribbon that tugged upon my insides. How she could paralyze me with a look and set me on a new course with a mere suggestion? She was a beautiful, strong weed that could and would grow anywhere.

The next morning Dr. Lawrence took me aside and told me that I would not need to watch Jane anymore since she was dismissed for "Unmentionable Acts," especially upon an old, blind man. I did not say a word. I wondered whether He punished us for deeds with lowly intentions or for no deeds at all. Was judgement parceled out? If so, then by whom?

"Some of the orderlies saw her stealing pennies from children," he whispered, his beard with a bit of egg, or something resembling egg, quivering when he spoke.

"But she was kind," I replied, thinking of Carrot, wondering about Jane's glances and untoward conduct toward Dr. Lawrence.

"When she was not otherwise engaged," he mumbled, mostly to himself. "She is to be replaced as soon as possible. I shall send the word out." He paused. "Alas, your good friend is here again."

I searched about the ward expectantly for Elizabeth's golden hair startled with light, her black dress repeating itself in the shadows. But I did not detect her voice, her arm sweeping the air as she made a point in her conversation. And then my eyes alighted upon the veteran, Richard Wellfield. He was back. His red whiskers were in the shape of overgrown bushes on each side of his face. His sad mouth became upturned when he saw me. His damaged hand, with its three remaining fingers, saluted as I came near.

I took his ravaged hand, saw my dark eyes and blanket of dark hair reflected in the large pupils of his green striped eyes. "What have you done now?"

"I wanted to see your face again." His colourless hair fell across his mouth and his complete hand brushed it away. "No, this time it is my stomach. A bad piece of mutton I think. Perhaps it is nothing. Still, a friend brought me here."

"I am not certain that my face alone might cure you. On the contrary..."

"Have you heard much about India?" he interrupted, and then he suddenly clutched his stomach and his features contorted.

"No." I released his hand and it flew toward his stomach.

Then he relaxed again. "After the Great Mutiny of 1857 there have been many people interested in reforming India, trying to make conditions more sanitary for the soldiers there, trying to clear up the problems, including boils all over men's bodies, and various civil, military and native conflicts. Many people believe a new war will break out there."

"Does this interest you?" I asked him.

"Yes, I want to travel there and be ready. Would it interest you there? They need nurses desperately and we could work together. We need not marry," he said haltingly, lowering his voice "unless you want to. But we are everlasting friends and could remain as such, are we not?"

"Yes, Richard Wellfield, we are fast friends. But I would need to think about this. This travelling. The sun can burn my limbs and I then feel too bedraggled to be of any use." Although there would be meaning to my life and I would not need to return home. The meaning would have to be my own. I had learned that beauty, and perhaps achievements, could also be illusions, just like Mr. Robert-Houdin's clever tricks.

But even Sleeping Beauty was an illusion, for does she not waken when kissed by the appropriate prince? She could not have been simply waiting but was cursed and therefore caught between two opposing or conflicting forces and suspended between the two opposites. She was in a gray area poised between right and wrong, good and bad. She did not know who she truly was, being suspended in time at such a young age. She would learn to discover herself. Unlike the Madonna in the engraving who already knew who she was but was uncertain about the person she gazed upon. She was not unlike me.

"A friend told me that during the war he had met Martin Farland. He said Martin was a good chap—a soldier who thawed men's frozen shirts and knocked down icicles upon the barracks windows in winter and carried men from the ships bringing the wounded that docked near the barracks. Until he, too, became ill."

"Yes, yes. That was my Martin." I, too, was a form of sleeping beauty. Or a liar waiting to wake up, caught between right and wrong.

A phrase Flo had said during the war drifted through my mind: listen to those dying around you.

I could hear the bony finger of a branch with slick, knotted buds tapping at the window, wanting to come in, be rescued, and be healed. I could hear it above the patients' voices, the thud of feet and clattering of basins and instruments, if I tried hard to listen. That day no one was dying in the ward. I crept to the window to see the white, papery heads of flowers, the narcissi, and the sky with its different shades of pink, blue, and mostly gray. The white smears of clouds unfolding like fresh laundry. The wounded sky was deciding whether it would rain later or not.

"I am sorry to make you so sad, Miss Russell," the veteran said, leaning back into his bed.

~

My room was deliciously empty of people and I could not hear anyone in the house. It was quiet, no servants or visitors going to and fro. I sank into the bed, feeling myself a dried leaf blown about by an autumn wind, unsure of any direction, ready to be scattered, dropped to bare ground, trampled by unknowing feet. I was tired. It seemed so long ago that I first came to the Thompson house but it had only been just over two months.

Rose's ceiling was smooth and white, and unlike the hospital, devoid of scars or stains. The air here was powdery and warm from being held in the empty room all day long. It was how I would have felt in my family house, caught. I would become a restless Mrs. Thompson. There would be no stillness, no privacy.

I let my hands kiss the air and dance. I pressed them together. Some voices murmured from downstairs, a man and a woman, some laughter. But they were faint and far away.

I got off the bed and opened a small chest in Rose's closet and saw handkerchiefs with "R" embroidered upon them. Also: a sewn doll with button eyes; hessian made into the shape of a horse; a dog with a torn paw; and a limp cat with a blue-ribboned collar. Loose pieces of paper had pen marks with large, unsteady "R"s and crude pictures of men with whiskers or women in flowing dresses. I closed the lid.

I removed paper from the desk and dipped and poised my pen above it but I could not begin. I knew I should not. My arm froze above the blank sheet of paper like a spirit at a se-ance about to enter a medium's body. I wondered whether Eliz-abeth's friend could hypnotize me so I would not think about Flo anymore. I was doubtful. I put the pen down. I believed we should all be skeptical of what is around us.

I poured some alcohol into two drinking-glasses and mixed some laudanum for Mrs. Thompson and myself. The red seep-ing, like blood at the barracks, was mixed and diluted through the colourless liquid. Soon it would become a part of my own blood.

Mrs. Thompson was weary, the stone of a dog at her feet. The bed conformed to her person, hugging her heavy body, the sheets wrapped about her usual nightclothes, her hair tucked beneath her bonnet. Candlelight flickered on and off of them, scribbling on them, making Mrs. Thompson and her dog appear large and suddenly small. The smell of cut flowers that have grown too old permeated her room, a rotting scent of browning petals and green stems left too long in water, growing thick and sticky. We both drank and set our drink-ing-glasses down together. As she went to sleep I removed the glasses and returned to my room.

I took comfort in a nurse's anonymity. Though people of-ten listened to me for instructions, many patients and relatives only noticed me during illness. Most did not know me at all. Neither patients nor their families ever truly saw me. They were thankful and then, when they were well, they did not need me any longer. There were so many sick people I could have spent my life tending to them if my mother and sister had allowed it. A part of me was tugged into their illness and pain and when they were done with their needs I was thrown back upon myself. I stared out the window at nothing but rain dripping from the roof, its sound a tapping all about the house, like a stranger knocking to enter.

I wondered if God knew my thoughts and helped to direct them. I knelt by the side of the bed in a manner I had not done since I was a child. I pressed my hands together as if clapping but without a sound. My elbows sank into the soft coverlets, my knees adjusted to the rug.

And then I realized that I did not need to maintain a certain position to speak to my God, that He would answer or not answer no matter how I had arranged my limbs. So I sat upon the bed and focused upon Him, although my mind wandered a bit. I remembered that Flo had said that her spirituality was not seances or trances, visions, or punishments, but was made manifest through work within this world. She wanted to lessen suffering through "mankind creating mankind." She wanted each person to experience the goodness of God themselves. She believed they could and she was right, for that was what had happened to me. I had experienced Him directly although I was in church when it occurred. Now I felt as if I were two people. One who maintained life and work in this world and another, somewhere else, and always available to receive His Word. Part of another world. I was distracted yet content also. I was always listening and waiting.

The rain beat upon the roof and windows, was a heart pushing against a patient's skin, blood coursing through a body. The lonely sound pulsed around me. There was no other noise now but the echo of the rain within my room and it was a music resembling a drum, a dripping I could lose myself within. It was like praying and I asked if what I had heard before, in the church, was correct, if what was meant was what was received. I asked again and again and realized that I was not lonely then, in the asking. The rain and I had a conversation. I fell asleep to the repetition of the rain, a book about Egypt open upon the table.

~

The next day I thought I glimpsed Mabel on Well Road near Hampstead. She appeared to be walking with a man who resembled Dr. Lawrence, with a beard and a black jacket. He nestled his hand in the hair upon his chin every so often, and it hid within that dark roughage only to emerge and return again like a burrowing animal. But, then, as I drew closer, it was not Dr. Lawrence. This man's eyes were narrower and his nose set lower upon his face. Just then a cab wheeled by between us; the horse was trotting and the carriage groaned and clanked. The horse's white, stringy mane flopped as it passed and when I looked up, Mabel and the bearded man were rounding a corner. I hurried behind them and walked at a slight distance, trying to listen. A cabbage butterfly halted its flight upon my shoulder, its wings pulsing, and then it flew off.

"Yes, Miss, would you do that for me?" the bearded man asked, his hands rushing into his black pockets, bulging there.

Mabel wore her sky blue dress and brown boots. Averting my eyes, I saw that her boots scurried like Mrs. Thompson's Chinese dog. Mabel wore a small brown bonnet and in her profile her sunken mouth was working to say something. "That there's something I'm acquainted with," nearly formal, in a voice not her own. "You'll have to cross my hand with several shillings."

"Yes," he said stiffly, "of course." And he pressed a walking stick ahead of him that I had not noticed before.

"First I'll need something to eat." She straightened her bonnet; her fingers spread upon it like pale spiders.

"How about a drink in this tavern?" He pointed with his stick.

"I don't drink no more. Just a little food first." And she pointed toward an eating establishment.

She took his arm and they disappeared inside the establishment, which was bustling. I waited outside and preoccupied myself for a while by watching the carriages and people pass. A house across the street had rags stuffed in the windows and smoke puffing into the sky, clouding it, forming the shapes of animals. Then a face like Mrs. Tatterspol came to a window, only younger, with a bright splotch of rouge upon her cheeks, and rings upon her fingers that caught the low light and sent it flying as if it were upon a trapeze. In another window a man's breeches hung upon a chair, a flag declaring surrender.

Next I concentrated instead upon a small front yard and saw a red rose bush trellised upon a gate, the flowers full and open, big, velvety wounds encased by greenery. Some spare, trodden grass. I watched a young lad dip his fingers into a woman's skirt pocket below her shawl and stuff something glittering into his own pocket. He sauntered off slowly, whistling, as if he had just finished playing with some mates. And I thought of the boy at the hospital, who claimed he would improve, and Jane, who might not. I felt unhappy about Jane's dismissal because I had liked her. I would have liked to tell Mabel all the hospital gossip, to which she would have replied, "Naw, they didn't, did they?"

I grew tired of waiting for Mabel so I wandered to a bookseller where I had been before. I pushed open the door to
browse through the travel books. Behind me was the sky with
its touch of blue fading to gray. As the door closed the slice
of pale sky grew thinner and the noise outside grew dim and
finally faded. I smelled the damp, moldy odour of books and
their covers, of the old wood that their spines rested upon.

"May I help you, Madam?" The bookseller was a bespeck-
led man with some sort of a fleshy growth upon his cheek the
size of a walnut. Possibly it was a tumor or a cyst. It was not
likely a mole or callus.

"I am looking for a book about India."

"Ah, all the rage now. Here is a lovely one, Madam." The
growth bobbed up and down as he spoke. He had a slight sour
smell about him as though he had slept among his own books,
had picked up their odour, was transforming into a book himself. He offered me a thick book. "Since the 1857 Great Mutiny
against Britain much has been written about that subconti-
nent—so much turmoil there."

I browsed through the pages with engravings of dark-
skinned men carrying water. In the middle pages a woman
with a hoop piercing her nose and more bangles upon her
wrists and feet than Mrs. Tatterspol balanced a jar upon her
head, held a gathering of straw as a broom in her hand. The
heat appeared overwhelming from the crisp pages of the book.
I thought of Flo and her concerns for sanitation for the soldiers
there. And how I wished to discuss India with her. There was
a sketch of Simla in Himalaya where the British went to escape
the summer heat of Calcutta. It was full of pink and white shut-
tered homes with fluffy balls of vegetation encroaching upon
their walls. It did not look too unpleasant there. But Calcutta

was dry, dusty, hot, and teeming with impoverished people whose bones pressed through their dark skin. They did not want the British there. There was the caste system, the Hindus, Muslims, Parsis, and Jains, cholera (my old acquaintance), the monsoons, the various dialects, the political bickering, famines, the vines that crawled through everything, rooting everywhere. I shut the tome with a gentle slap.

"Are you interested in purchasing it, Madam?"

I could not see his growth when I stood to his right and his profile was pleasing from that side. "No," I said. "Perhaps another time." The sky opened again to me with its clusters of clouds, the drifting gray petals of almost-light. The busy London street rose up and greeted me again.

# Invitations

Mrs. Thompson had sufficiently recovered from her dreadful fright precipitated by Mrs. Tattersol's fall and death and now screeched at Mary to quicken her steps to come and help her dress for her first social outing in a long time. The little Chinese dog, Fu, yapped and leaped about her feet, as she stood by the doorway. A black, shiny dress without puffs gloved her full figure and was hanging from her shoulders unbound, a rind peeling from fruit. Beads clustered about her neck like flies. A row of hidden buttons was revealed, punctuating the blackness, a row of teeth marks. I could see her stockinged feet and the slit of her flesh down her back reaching down to her underclothes. Pearl earrings shuddered at her ears as she yelled and her necklace jumped against her throat, protesting Mary's laziness. Her gray hair was yet undone and shook about her neck.

Mary ran into the room and gathered Mrs. Thompson's hairbrush and began to brush her hair. She held the gray tresses over her arm as if she were holding a piece of valuable cloth. Mary's own hair was tied back and patted down and flat against her head.

"Thank goodness you finally came. I have the Poorhouse Ball tonight and I shall see Mrs. Oberlin there." The dog pawed at her hem. "Stop it," she said to the bobbing fur of his head. Mary busied herself with Mrs. Thompson's hair, twisting and braiding it and affixing it to the top of her head. "James," she yelled. "That boy is never here anymore. He is too busy to escort me anywhere," she said to a subdued Mary. "Ann," she tried lastly.

And I came to her from the hallway expectantly, having listened to the complete repertoire of names she had already employed. I could not miss hearing and seeing it all through her open door.

"Ann," she said with a sweet lilt to her voice, "perhaps I need some medicine to liven me up from my illness and carry me through the evening. Do you have anything like that?"

"Why, yes, Mrs. Thompson. I shall fetch it." I went to the kitchen and stirred a piece of cooked beet in a glass of water. No one saw me, but if they had, I would not have cared. The water turned a thin, red-pink colour and when Mrs. Thompson drank it down in three large gulps she said, "This medicine has a slight earthy, sweet taste."

"Yes," I said, "it is strong and should work quickly."

~

I would continue what I had begun. I would tend to the suffering of others. Richard Wellfield's invitation to go to India passed through my mind and yet, was it the right thing to do? I was not certain. I would try to work magic with the body or at least the illusion of it. And I realized Mrs. Tatterspol had been correct—that we were alike.

At the hospital there was a rank smell that my lavender perfume could not hide. The young lad's head was swathed in white bandages stabbed with red streaks, yet he was healing well, his fever abating and then blossoming again. After three weeks his eyesight was faltering and he began to address me as "My Dim Angel." I now realized that there were different layers of consciousness and reality. There was the war and Flo, Mr. Robert-Houdin, seances, hypnosis, and laudanum. Which layer was the fairies or Sleeping Beauty? The young lad was caught within one layer under the surface while he was healing. He became delirious for some time. He would weep with abandon over a scrap of food, turning it over and over in his hands, or his failing eyes met mine. Often I was busy and was not able to see him much. With Jane gone, Dr. Lawrence and I tended to the patients as best we could.

The veteran took my hand in his damaged one and looked kindly and longingly at me. I knew he was waiting for my decision. He had trimmed his reddened muttonchops into the shape of a sideways chair. But he did not stir my heart.

Dr. Lawrence only had time to bark orders at me. And I took orders well. I gave plates splotched with dollops of gray and brown food to the veteran and the boy. The veteran did not want to eat on account of his stomach cramping and the lad drifted in and out of sleep and could not stay awake long enough to eat his dull coloured food. I spooned the wet, brown mush into his small, open mouth and he began to eat and swallow a bit.

Somehow the hospital and the Thompson house began to merge—the people from one place spilling and appearing in the other. I believed I saw a hospital kitchen lad in the Thompson scullery one evening. And once I thought I saw James strolling about the hospital garden, picking flowers leisurely, his blonde hair one long piece of sunlight falling around his face. I wondered whether the flowers would become a bouquet for me. Yet when I looked outside again he was gone. Perhaps it was not actually James—just as I thought I had seen Dr. Lawrence before. The big difference between the two places was that the patients at the hospital were truly sick while Mrs. Thompson had the illness of her class, not enough to keep her occupied.

Curiously I found myself missing Mabel and slipping down to the cellar as though I would still find her there. That surprised me. And the silence in the cellar and lack of any scurrying rats somehow displeased me. The kitchen was busy as usual but it lacked the subterranean knowledge that Mabel possessed and dispensed, alternately the stomach and seat of gossip of the hospital. I hesitated upon the steps, expecting her ghostly hands to emerge and clutch the rails, telling me what had become of poor Jane, begging for a bit of food. I had never gone hungry, eaten rats.

But I had eaten other things. I supposed that no matter how well we each believed we knew ourselves there were still discoveries.

In the afternoon I helped the young, aspiring pickpocket drink a cup of water. Underneath his bandages his head had mostly healed and the tender skin was uneven and lumpy. The hair would grow back later. I did not believe that he would grow up looking too peculiar. He appeared to be past infection.

"My Dim Angel," he said squinting, then finding and holding the glass unsteadily with his two hands. "You're back to tend to me. I'll find you a special gift when I'm out of here." He still had a crooked, child's smile.

"You are very sweet," I said taking the glass away, "but I do not want for anything just now."

Dr. Lawrence advanced upon the bed and interrupted us. Blood was splattered upon his apron. He held his wet hand high in the air as though he were about to wave. His beard was twisted to his right side. "A little drummer boy and his friend with one leg brought this for you this morning. I had nearly forgotten." He reached into his jacket pocket with his other hand and gave me an envelope.

I was both excited and nervous. I ran to a chair beneath the print of the Madonna who gazed upon my head placidly and soothingly. I opened the letter with much anticipation and read:

*My Dear Ann,*

*I should so like to see you as you have requested and have made an appointment to do so in two weeks, Wednesday at three in the afternoon. Some days I am unfit to see visitors, even my beloved nurses and friends from the war who are so dear to my heart, but I am hoping to be well enough on that day. I am trying to keep my strength for His work and believe such strife can bring us nearer to a one-ness with God. I think of what St. Catherine said—"God became man in order to make man into God."*

*I am happy that you are devoted still to nursing and that you are helping our dear children. Whatever the Lord has desired of us we cannot refuse Him. I do not want to regard myself too much and listen to Him too little.*

*Do not allow the goings-on in the Thompson house or anywhere else to distract you from your work. It will be pleasing to see a face from the Crimea. It has been a long time.*

*"It is I. Be not afraid."*

*Yours, Flo*

I folded the letter and tucked it into my apron where it rustled as I walked. I pressed my fingertips to the cheeks of the Madonna. I was elated. I would see Flo in two weeks. I could not stop from smiling. I straightened my hair, which was pulled back, showing my scalp as a white line in the center of my head that disappeared beneath my nurse's cap. I could feel my heart beating, pressing against my ribcage, pushing at my skin. The tiny, excited leaping. An eddy of blood outside its usual quietude, the difficulty of holding my heart in the place where it belonged.

The veteran was snoring but I woke him by pulling one of the fingers that was left upon his hand. His eyes opened and my chin rested upon my throat as I leaned into his chest covered by blankets.

"I cannot go with you to India. All that matters to me is here, in England, and I cannot leave."

His eyelids fluttered, yet he was not astonished. "I will miss speaking to you, Miss Russell," he managed. "I have always held you in the highest regard." His sad mouth grew sadder.

"I know, Richard Wellfield, I know. I will miss our talks as well."

~

I left the hospital early and went through the hall at the Thompson house where a grandfather clock chimed the time for tea. A Venetian glass vase upon a nearby table shook at the clock's loud noise. A bluebottle fly buzzed about a painting upon the wall called "The Luncheon" by Cooper/Shenton in which two men ate with their two hungry dogs in attendance, two horses waiting patiently in the background. The fly settled upon the hilly, bare earth that amiably reflected the roiling sky. I went past the chandelier that fractured light into the shape of trembling foliage and entered my room. I began a letter to Flo filled with my thoughts and all that had happened since I had last written.

*In the last month in London I have attended a reading, a wax museum, seances, and tried to fall in love. None of it has stuck.*

I crumpled the paper and tossed it aside.

I began again: *I have never wanted for anything—except you. I have had my work, when I have been allowed to practice it. My mother and sister have long been opposed to what I do best; though if the social situation suits them, I am allowed to practice nursing. I have not yet married. I may never.*

*I still miss the war—but not the deaths of so many soldiers, all our children. Merely the purpose and need of it. I miss learning from you.*

*And after such a long silence I have heard from my God. He told me, "Continue." I have continued to relieve suffering, to look to Him for direction and help. It is heartening to make that which is mystical or spiritual into an outward form. It has long been a question and I received a brief answer. I believe I can live up to it and follow it and it is enough. I want to infuse the spiritual within my life and the life of others. I have been teetering so long, on the brink of going so many different ways...I suppose I have always wanted to be you.*

And then I tossed that letter aside also.

I began a shorter note: *Thank you for your invitation and appointment. Seeing you again means much to me, especially since I am aware how limited your time and energy and health are these days.*

*You are often in my thoughts and I will always remember your*

*extraordinary kindness during the war. I am looking forward to seeing
such a dear old friend again soon. There is much to tell you.*

*Ever yours, Ann*

I slipped this letter into an envelope and asked Mary to
deliver it. It was already evening and Mrs. Thompson had left
for another of her social engagements, a benefit for orphaned
children. Mary said that Mrs. Thompson wore her black skirt
and shawl, dark curtains closed over her plump figure.

Mary's hair bristled against my door as she said that the
boy would send it out immediately. I realized that her disar-
rayed hair reminded me of my life.

"I saw my Hera last night. My pet owl that died when I
left for the Crimea." Mary looked at me strangely but she had
been privy to most of my life in the Thompson house. "It was a
dream," I confided to her. "I was walking by snowy mountains
surrounded by a blue sky and blue water below. I wanted to
catch her but her white wings spread and she caught a breeze
out of my reach."

"Yes, Miss," she said. "There've been too many strange goings-on in this house lately." She grimaced as she went out the
door.

## The Not Visible

At the Thompson house, two servants were cleaning up the plates from the simple meal James and I had just enjoyed, one of fish, potatoes, and bread. He and I moved to the parlour, passing the rooted countenances of his ancestors staring at us from their stately paintings. A bronze statue of a ballerina danced on the mantelshelf before us, next to a clock. Mrs. Thompson was not expected back until late from her dinner. James lit a cedar spill in the fireplace and used it to light his cigar. The fire reared up in complicity and spit. As he did so, the flame illuminated his face and I could feel the dark, empty space of the room around us. Yet I did not light any candles. I settled into a dark, overstuffed chair that I remembered was maroon in the daylight. I imagined the birds and flowers sleeping, closed up and curled into themselves, if that was what they did, or else befuddled by the end of the world. In the moonlight, clouds scudded by the window like ghosts late for a seance. James poured a brandy and gazed at the empty ceiling. A pitcher sat near him on a table.

"I have heard that in some places electricity is being employed to heal the sick," I said, and his blonde hair fanned as he turned around.

He sat upon the sofa, the not unpleasant cigar smoke mingling with smoke from the fire. "Let me show you something."

He went to his room and retrieved a thick, heavy glass rod and his fur-lined cloak. He laid out bits of torn paper upon a table and rubbed the glass rod with the fur. He held the rod near the paper and the bits flew to the rod and attached themselves there. He returned the objects to his room and sat down, picking up his cigar and drinking-glass again. He looked at the argument of the fire. "The glass rod was changed by the fur and could, therefore, pick up the paper. I believe electricity is an inherent property of matter. As to its healing qualities, that I do not know about."

"Yet that is the part that interests me."

"Women do not often understand the full implications of certain matters but are only able to see the pieces." He sipped at his drink, his hair brushing his ears. "Important events. How glass can be used by electricity and gain other desirable properties."

"I believe we are like men in that we pursue that which interests us."

He leaned back into the darkened arms of the sofa, his hair fringing the edges, the rest of him invisible. I began to feel restless.

"Perhaps you are right, Pain. But I wish women would think more about what they do before they do it, at least particular members of your sex." He swished his brandy and the cigar glowed at his mouth. "I put much time and thought into my scientific experiments."

I did not believe that we were discussing the experiments any longer. "Yes, I am certain that you do."

~

As I retired that evening, I undressed in front of the child's looking-glass, not much larger than a piece of writing paper. It was often difficult undoing the backs of clothes and under-clothes, the materials peeling from me, revealing the dark spar-rows of my eyes darting from edge to edge. The surface of the looking-glass revealed the arc of a neck, a drizzle of candlelight across my shoulders and the top of my breast where the skin began to curve and showed where my flesh was wrought into lines from the corset. The lines were remembering the press of my undergarments, and were now fleshing out, no longer thralled, my own blossoming. My face flew whitely backwards as my hand grazed my bosom and stayed there, then moved on. A delicious mistake. My legs were cold, surrounded by the pile of my clothes and undergarments and yet unspeakably open. An arrested smile arrived upon my lips that was not mine. I thought of Elizabeth and her beauty and the yellow softness of her hair and kissing, and James and his electric hands, the way he caught my arm, and Flo with her excitable mind, her champagne-coloured hair, her strident calves. And the bird of my face lifted toward the sky and vanished, returning to its source, and sang. A moth had been caught within me and had severely battered against my ribcage and I had finally let it go.

Sweat showed itself at my forehead and I wiped it away. I wondered briefly whether I was a sexual opportunist, a bit like Elizabeth, or merely confused. It was not worth an old spinster's contemplation. I contentedly slipped into my nightclothes and stood by the small bed. Something was missing. I opened a chest in the closet and removed the hessian horse, the dog with the ragged paw with cloth issuing from its cut and the doll with black button eyes that felt flat and empty and stared at me coldly and distantly. I stuffed the hair I had collected from the

newly dead into the wound of the dog and closed the cut. I put
them all back except for the poor dog, which I took to my bed
to heal. I placed the dog gently beneath the covers and crawled
beside it and held its mangled paw. I fell asleep thinking of the
startled face of the moon outside my window turning to the
resting flowers and dark, bent grass for comfort.

~

I was awakened that night by a muffled bustling downstairs but I did not stir immediately. Then there were shrill
cries and cursing and I thought of the war and the wounded
carried into the hospital. I bolted upright in bed as the poor
stuffed dog fell upon the floor and lay there forlorn and askew.
I heard my name called. "Ann, Ann, come quickly." Then the
rush of feet at my door and the agitated entrance of Mary, her
hair disheveled, a candle in her hand and her shadow menac-
ing upon the wall.

"Come quickly. It's Mrs. Thompson," she cried and hurried
out.

I returned the dog to the chest and ran downstairs in my
nightclothes. Mary and two servants, also in their nightclothes,
were carrying Mrs. Thompson through the front door.  Mrs.
Thompson was screaming at first but then she quieted and
her head grew slack and her tongue lolled and hung from her
mouth. At first I could not see what the problem was, but then
I saw her dangling legs and much blood, dark red upon her
black clothes, so it blended in and could not be seen. There was
a trail of blood, a rain of blood, splattered upon the floor like
spilt coins. I smelled earth and meat and dampness.

"The doctor has been sent for and is coming," Mary said.

"Where is James?"

"I don't know," Mary answered. "He's not in his bedchamber and hasn't been all night."

"Put her down upon the breakfast table."

And they rushed her in and placed her upon the table. I examined Mrs. Thompson and saw that the leg bone had cracked and had pierced the skin below her knee and she was bleeding profusely. Thankfully she was no longer awake as I wrapped linens tightly about her leg to stop the bleeding. The first linen soaked with blood quickly and became soft so I made another and tightened it upon her leg. The other leg was badly bruised but otherwise seemed uninjured.

"What happened?"

Mary said, "I heard a horse whinny outside the house just as Mrs. Thompson got home. Then the horse and carriage took off and I heard a thump. Then there was screaming. I think the horse struck Mrs. Thompson."

Dr. Carroll arrived with his spectacles at an odd, crooked angle. His frock was unbuttoned, his trousers kneaded and creased. His whitened hair spilled over his collar and stuck out into the air. I was glad he had arrived so soon. Mary had brought in an oil lamp and straightened the dining table and the area around it. Dr. Carroll inspected Mrs. Thompson and quickly opened his bag. He took a small cotton ball, placed it in a wire cage, then poured ether over it and positioned the apparatus over Mrs. Thompson' mouth and nose. He told everyone to leave save Mary and myself.

"It is good that you were a nurse in the Crimea and that you were here to staunch the bleeding, but the leg is broken in too many places." He unwound the bloody linens and pushed her clothes higher so they formed black clouds suspended over her pale, unmoving body. It was indecent but necessary. "For the leg will have to be removed immediately."

Mary nearly fainted at those words and she placed one hand upon my shoulder and whispered, "I don't know if I can be of much help."

I briefly thought that Mrs. Thompson would now have an affliction to truly worry about.

Mrs. Thompson's black underclothes were visible and sliced showing a white V of flesh, which began to seep through the openings in her tight corset. Dr. Carroll placed his instruments upon the table, knives, clamps, two saws, linens, and the can of ether if we needed more. He first used a tourniquet to stop the flow of blood. When he began to cut through the skin and the layers beneath it with a scalpel, hitting bone, Mary fainted dead away upon the floor. I did not have time to move her but had to step over her until I could push her toward the wall. There was much blood and the noise of the capital saw through bone was terrible, a hard, grating sound that seemed to echo. Then a slight snap. We were grateful that Mrs. Thompson remained unconscious and did not need more ether. Dr. Carroll applied pressure and then sutured her leg with dark silk. We were not certain she would live or be able to regain her strength. Dr. Carroll suspected that she might have broken a bone in her ribcage also. We bandaged her leg and below her chest, and generally stopped the bleeding. This was much more care than the men received in the Crimea.

I pushed the reclining figure of Mary against the wall, leaving red handprints upon her clothes and a large, wet streak across the floor. I threw a blanket over Mrs. Thompson's indecent parts and we carried her upstairs with the aid of two servants and laid her upon her own bed. I could hear the little

Chinese dog, Fu, crying and barking downstairs, locked in a room. I arranged for someone to watch Mrs. Thompson at all times and to call me for any movement or more bleeding. I would run to the hospital in a few hours and fetch an amputation pillow and other supplies.

"You must get some sleep, Miss Russell. You have much work ahead of you," Dr. Carroll said. "You must change her dressing every few hours and use a poultice when it is needed."

Mrs. Thompson was no one's property now. Not that she ever was. It would have been difficult to imagine. I tried to wipe some of the blood from Dr. Carroll's frock and shirt before he left but I merely rubbed it into larger splotches. He was very tired. "I hope all is going well for you at St. Thomas's hospital, Miss Russell."

"Yes, it is. Thank you, Dr. Carroll."

~

That night my dream of Martin Farland returned but it was not Martin whose face loomed and begged to die, nor did he watch me do the surgeon's job on another boy whose blood formed its own red ocean. The face grew larger as it drew nearer and his lips opened and he did not ask to die but said, "I must die in order to be reborn." It was not Martin, it was my father, his white hair feathered as it was just before he died. And in my dream I asked him, "Must you?" But he did not answer and I awoke with a start.

It was still night outside. I circled on a rug in my bare feet as though chasing my own shadow, apparitions seemed to twist around me. I paused at the window to see stars following the partial moon. The sky was comfortable, quiet. Then a strong wind outside made everything alive and noisy, with tree branches arching and brushing the outside walls. Something shook upon the roof. The loud voice of the wind whistled through cracks, entering the house any way it could. The crying of the yet-to-be-born. "Very well," I whispered to no one in particular. The wind answered in a peculiar language, one I could not understand.

~

The next morning I checked on Mrs. Thompson and changed her bandages as she lay asleep. She seemed pale as she had lost much blood. I took a hansom cab to hasten my journey to the hospital. I thought of all the men rushing to find gold in America; even before the war I had read about them. They arrived in hordes by wagon train or steam train, or on horseback. I read how so many sacrificed themselves and their animals for gold fever and were still doing so, according to the newspapers. It was ridiculous. Mrs. Thompson had enough riches and gold and still was unwell and unhappy. I wondered what they believed they would really find—their unanswered dreams? The cab shook and creaked like my sister scolding me. I held onto the seat.

When I arrived, Dr. Lawrence was lancing a boil on an old woman's hand, which shook in anticipation of the knife.

"I can't look," the woman said, turning her wrinkled face away.

"It is good that you are here, Miss Russell." His beard swayed between his shoulders and hung down as he made his cut. "I daresay we need the help, although we have just hired another nurse. I believe you are acquainted with her." The poison oozed out. "You will be quite surprised to see her." He held out the knife for me to take away but I was not paying attention, wondering who the new nurse could be. Instead it pierced the tender flesh below my thumb and before the second finger of my right hand. It stung as the small wound began to bleed. I grasped the knife, wiped it with a rag, and placed it with his other medical instruments.

"Oh dear," was all I could say. "I am here to fetch an amputation pillow and medicines as Mrs. Thompson has had an amputation. I will not be able to stay long when I come. I am glad you have another nurse and I should be happy to meet her."

"I am sorry to hear about Mrs. Thompson. Perhaps at a more opportune time you can tell me what happened." He wiped off his hands with another rag.

And then a sudden sharp pain in my abdomen bent me near to the floor.

He reached down to right me and his eyebrows grew closer. He peered at my hand. "I fear that your wound may grow worse and I am concerned with your stomach area. Perhaps you should stay here for a little while and we will watch for a fever or infection or further pains." He motioned to an empty bed near the young pickpocket who was sleeping soundly and said, "You must rest here a while and we will tend to you for a change."

Dr. Lawrence hurried off to another patient. But I felt suddenly better as my stomach pain subsided. I threw the removed boil, wrapped in rags, into a container for such things. And I went to the apothecary cabinet, shot through with light this morning so that it formed rainbows of blue, green, and red upon the blank walls and scuffled floor. My hand passed

through the colours forming in the air and it turned half blue
and half green for a moment. I soaked up the thin stream of
my blood with a rag as I chose a thick amputation pillow suitable for Mrs. Thompson. I did not want to leak my blood and
stain the medical supplies but my wound was still open and
gaping like a small, red mouth and I dabbed at it. I left bloody
thumbprints upon the bottle of opium powder and attempted
to wipe them off, as there had been too much blood spilt lately.
My hand ached a bit with all the movement.

I prepared a poultice for the patient with the boil and a
small one for my own wound to try and stave off infection for
both. I followed the anxious birds of light skittering upon the
floor and walls back into the ward and gently placed the poultice upon the patient.

"Go to your sick bed," Dr. Lawrence barked at me as I
passed him.

I placed the supplies at the foot of the bed and lay on top
of the freshly cleaned bedsheets. I propped the pillow with my
left hand and waited for aches or an infection to come upon
me. I held my poultice over my wound whose bleeding was
slowed. I did not like feeling so useless and helpless and hated
wasting time to wait for an illness to occur. I would not mind
fever and pain if I knew it would pass and that I would then
live. I knew that stomach pain could be from many different
illnesses. I had not fallen ill during the war as so many other
nurses and doctors had. Flo had succumbed to sickness there
and it had not left her. I wondered who the new nurse tending
to me would be. A friend of Flo's? Someone from the war days?
Victoria from another ward at St. Thomas's? What Dr. Lawrence
had said intrigued me. The young pickpocket moved his raw
head that had healed nicely so far, his eyes stammered open,

he said, "My Dim Angel." His face cracked with a smile.

I smiled also. "I have joined you now." A pulsing pain shot through my hand briefly.

He peered at my hand. "But it's so small as to be nothing."

"I hope so," I answered. I glanced at my wound and the bleeding had stopped so I lifted off the poultice. There was not much swelling nor had my pains returned. I imagined fever and poisoning would be like the effects of laudanum: some bleakness, rich colours, form eclipsed by other forms, my logic furiously gone, the sun, the moon, my eyes and head would ache in sympathy, dim shapes claiming and reclaiming the world, the heat of India, a sheen of perspiration dampening my arms and neck and chest. I realized it was one thing to tend to patients with fever and another thing to have and feel pain and fever. I did not want to be delirious, especially before Dr. Lawrence and the staff.

It was then that Mabel entered the ward, her nurse's cap jaunty, bouncing upon her head, an apron wrapped about her brown dress, her boots peeking out and stomping hard upon the floor. "Why, if it ain't Ann, my savior." She came to my bed. She gazed upon my wound. "Is that why you're laying about this bed?"

"Yes," I told her, shocked to see her. "And Dr. Lawrence ordered me here for a while to see if I had some further stomach pains. The wound is from a small surgery that he performed."

"Hmm. It's a little, bitty thing but we could blister ya if ya catch the fever or sweat the poison out from the blood." Her hair shone neatly pulled back beneath her cap.

"How did you learn that? What are you doing here, Mabel? I am surprised to see you."

"I know a bit about nursing and I'm learning more as I go

along here." Her sunken mouth gaped, exposing few teeth. "But I needed a job and I missed it here. This way I kin visit my friends downstairs if there's any left."

She reached out for my hand but I flinched and pulled it close to my body and did not want her to touch it. I was not certain I wanted to work with Mabel, to allow her to try to heal me. I did not want her bony fingers clawing at my hand as if it held food there. Yet, then, when she picked it up and held it and inspected it, I did not mind. I did rather like her and hoped for more for her as well. "We'll see how it goes."

I lay against my pillow, my hand resting upon my abdomen, which was no longer tender and had grown calm. I watched Mabel as she checked the pickpocket's injury, as she cleaned tabletops and collected the washing and wrung out rags, as she mixed some medicines, handing them carefully to Dr. Lawrence. As she passed me by she said, "I've got a room a me own now."

I was restless watching her do all the work, my nursing work that should have been my own. "I am feeling quite well now." She was not terrible at it either. She spilt some medicines and sometimes dropped a rag or a square of linen, a basin slopped, or she hurried a patient while tapping her foot impatiently as though she were listening to music. No one seemed distressed by her brusque movements. She was not kind or gentle and she did not take a patient's hand often but no one died from her ministrations either. I watched her upbraid the pickpocket. She told him not to move about so much, which was difficult for a lad of his age. She was very good at the upbraiding portion of nursing work.

"Don't be a bloody little fool of a lad," she shouted him down.

I wondered whether the exchange caused more of a hubbub with the boy than if he had risen and played with a friend.

"What do ye know," he protested.

"I'll feed ye to the rats."

And then he was quiet in his bed and he did not say any more to Mabel, who smoothed back her hair in victory. He had most likely heard rumors concerning Mabel, having stayed in the hospital so long.

It was soon time for food and the odours wafted up from the kitchen. Potatoes, and an unnamable meat. I often tried to guess what the meat was and I was often wrong. It did not make me hungry. But Mabel began smacking her lips as she assisted Dr. Lawrence at the inspection of a woman who looked to be with child. A young, scrawny woman with ill-humoured features.

I did not want to remain in bed much longer as the fever or pain did not appear to be declaring itself. I needed to attend to Mrs. Thompson or help Dr. Lawrence and Mabel. I did not need to gaze at the print of the Madonna but I did and she appeared to be crying, huge, yellowed tears that meandered down her cheeks. Could she have come to life at the hospital? Was she about to step from the engraving and help us with the patients? Were our ministrations that good? Did Mabel affront her or admonish her and make her cry? Was she crying for the child or me? Her red dress lost pieces of its colour in small streaks. Had I finally achieved a fever and the Madonna was the subject of my hallucinations? I stared at my hand with the wound and it had closed into a red slash and it wavered, blurred, and became a rat's paw stretched upon my bed. It was no longer part of my body and I wished it gone.

Perhaps I was dead already. Perhaps I had been dead for

a long time. I needed a new life. Mabel came and felt the skin on my cheeks and forehead and made a sour face. She had brought a damp rag that she plastered onto my forehead where it felt wet and cool.

"Ya don need this. You're healthy and ya can leave when ya want."

I peeled off the rag and felt my own skin with my left hand and it felt cool and there was no perspiration. I touched my abdomen and there was no pain. She was right and was not deluded. I sighed and rested back upon my pillow.

I watched Mabel devour the meals that the patients did not eat. But what she did was no worse than Jane and then the food was not wasted. She slipped some of it into rags that she tucked into her apron pockets and they bulged. Her sunken mouth chewed even after she had eaten. I began to point a finger at the engraving of the Madonna but Mabel came to the bed and pushed my arm down. She looked at the print.

"There've been leaks from the roof in the hospital. That picture might be destroyed." She shook her head.

I leaped out of bed and gathered the medicines and pillow for Mrs. Thompson. I did not make a good patient. "Thank you, Dr. Lawrence and Mabel, for your care. I shall look forward to seeing you both soon." And I could not leave quickly enough.

# Flo

When I returned from the hospital, Mrs. Thompson was lying quite still in her bed. A pillow tumbled from my arms into the place where her Chinese dog had often sat, before the accident. It was late in the day and the room was filled with the odours of perfume, blood, and fresh rags. A web of feeble stars was beginning at the window. Candlelight nuzzled the useless gloves and dresses and shoes waiting in Mrs. Thompson's wardrobe. A pair of earrings sparkled upon her dressing table in the center of the circle of her toiletry bottles. The bottles were arranged like music upon a page with its grids and lines and dots. All was quiet, except for Mary arranging a smattering of flowers in a vase, her loose hair knocking petals onto a table. When I gave Mrs. Thompson her medicine she began to moan and be delirious. In the voice of a crow she mumbled about "the madness seen in an eyelid," and "a longing for the empty spaces left by warm bodies," and "an orange carriage path trailing behind the wheels." She called for her husband, and for the cool, soothing hand of Mrs. Tatterspol. I offered my hand and she took it. I rubbed the newly scratched skin above her fingers, still braided with dirt. I would wash her with a cloth and basin of water later. "My leg," she cried out in a small child's voice and clutched at her invisible limb. "It is wracked with pain." Then our silence.

I felt slightly unwell myself as I tended to Mrs. Thompson that night. James did not return to the house. My own wound, minor by comparison, had begun to heal without any consequences but it hurt a bit when the skin was brushed or pulled by actions or gestures. Now it was the time of the month when my stomach ached and I was slow and thick and filled with sod. A root of blood spread within me. I grew tired and foggy. I placed a warm cloth at my middle while I watched Mrs. Thompson's pale body thrash as fish did when pulled from water. I held her limbs down if she buckled into herself too much, her half of a leg pointing out toward the door as if to escape, ending too soon upon her body, an unfinished painting, quivering in the air. Mrs. Thompson began to heal, though so slowly at first that I was uncertain whether she would die or not. Her body continued to grow skin and dry and close upon itself in the meanwhile.

Mary helped all she could, as her other duties had lessened a bit. She took to wearing a tiny cross around her neck, two small dashes of wood tethered together with a piece of dark blue yarn. Often, if she was busy tidying up, it stuck to the shoulder of her dress or was attached to her sleeve. She began to fuss with Mrs. Thompson's bedclothes and I plucked the cross from her back and let it fall back across her bosom. She noticed it had returned to swinging between her shoulders.

"It's for Mrs. Thompson. I'm hoping she'll get better." Her hands were still wringing.

"I have always wondered how much of ourselves we put into our possessions," I said, thinking of Rose's toys, my medicine chest, Mrs. Thompson's house. I did not have much else except what I had left at my family home. A favorite, worn piano, a bone comb with my initials, and Hera, my companion, who was long gone. My possessions had never represented my beliefs or me as they had for others. I had so few and they seemed to slip away so easily. "But it is a good idea, Mary. Perhaps we should pray." I had never done this before when a patient was ill, believing more in science.

Mrs. Thompson was quiet and appeared to be calm and sleeping. Mary and I knelt on opposite sides of her bed, our faces hidden and bent toward our hands. I asked my God how active we were in our own fates or destinies. Could I change the course of history, through my own history, for example? But I inquired without moving my lips. I asked with my mind while Mary murmured at the other side of the bed. I was too aware of her and her beseeching, small voice with its never-ending flat tone. Her prayers interrupted my prayers, making it difficult and annoying. Nonetheless I carried on. Suddenly I felt a frigid wind across my shoulders, but when I looked, the window was shut. My skirt swished in the cold air and the hair along my arms was raised. I thought of Mrs. Tatterspol and her cold, jabbering bracelets, her large hands upon my back, the bronchial spread of her dead fingers. I asked if Hera would come back to me in one form or another. There was no answer. Then I asked for a speedy recovery for Mrs. Thompson.

I could see our reflections in a magenta pitcher, all three curled into ourselves, dappled with candlelight, so small in the much larger world surrounding us, too tiny to be noticed. Or heard. Mrs. Thompson's delirium returned and Mary was called back to the kitchen. I was not certain that our Gods were the same, for Mary found it necessary to repeat herself and use a supplicating, imploring tone as though she were attempting to speak to a hard-of-hearing child. I knew my God was busy, did not need incantations, or to be spoken to in a childish manner. He would answer when it was the correct time to do so.

I watched Mrs. Thompson dappled by candlelight. Gone
was her boredom and scheming, her evenings of listless vio-
lins, cavernous ballrooms, velvet dresses, expensive wine, and
chandeliers with prismatic light, exotic fruit. She was awash
in her body, lost within its defined structure. Her wrists gal-
loped in the air. She gulped and moaned and her eyes flew
wide open. She stared at me and then at her legs. "It is really
gone then," she said quite lucidly, looking at her missing leg. "I
thought so." She clutched at her blanket. "Is James busy?"

"Yes."

"I do not know whether I can live like this."

"You will get better." Adapt, but I did not say this. Darwin's new theory. For she had lapsed again into delirium and
began tossing her head against her pillow and crying out. She
had found a moment of pure clarity in the midst of her illness.
It happened that way sometimes.

~

The dark trees grew vivid as morning crept toward us outside the window. I began counting the leaves on the largest
tree but I soon became tired and sat back to enjoy their green-
ness, grass crushed under a pony's hoof or the colours of a
vast ocean. I had slept but very little. Mrs. Thompson had been
feverish most of the night and fussed occasionally, although
she had been sedated. We would know more about her health
within the next day.

James arrived and appeared dazed and disheveled, his
clothes wrinkled and poorly fitting, his fair hair splayed and
dirty.

"I will sit with her now. You are free to go, Pain." He touched my arm gently, though not in annoyance. "Thank you," he said.

I wanted to ask him where he had been but fatigue overtook me and I was relieved to go. Mrs. Thompson was lying in her bed most peacefully now. Queer lumps of candle wax, fat, round onions, surrounded the two empty candleholders. As if the candles had leaked out and assumed another form, been transformed. James smelled of wet wool and smoke. It was a queer smell. All appeared queer to me that morning in my tired state.

I retired to my bed and placed a warm cloth upon my stomach. The aches were subsiding. A music box sat upon a small table and I wondered at its song, since I had not yet heard it. I felt myself changing, becoming attracted to subjects other than science, to poetry and religion and spiritual development. My father had introduced me to those areas of study but I had not pursued them as I had pursued science, especially the healing arts. I knew I was reaching within myself as formerly I was often reaching outside myself and cared more how others felt. I could see now how science and the other arts were wedded, somehow combined to create a fuller truth. But was I ready to see Flo again? It had been over ten years since I saw her last, yet she was always with me like an everyday dress. I glanced at the thin, red smile of my hospital wound, pleased that it had not developed into a fever and that it did not hurt too greatly with all the work I had left to do.

I studied the pattern of morning light upon the ceiling; white chrysanthemums exploded onto the walls. I could feel their bursting delight. I watched as the shadows hid in ornate tables and as the darkness in the corners of the room grew smaller. I wondered why nothing grew in the deep shadows of trees and bushes. Perhaps Darwin's adaptable plants had not arrived there yet. Then I fell fast asleep.

~

I awoke shortly and went in to check upon James and Mrs. Thompson, both of whom had fallen soundly asleep. Mrs. Thompson was snoring and, for once, I was relieved at such a sound. James was slumped into a chair with his legs tossed over the edge, his arms hanging from the rests, and his head thrown backwards. A stripe of light lay diagonally across his chest. His new smell of dry wool and faint smoke filled the room, suppressing Mrs. Thompson's smell of iron blood and the damp insides of an old squash. I quietly changed her bandages and tiptoed out of the room without waking either of them.

I was very much awake for some unknown reason, having had little sleep. I went in to the parlour and Mary brought me tea, steaming and fragrant. Though I faced the window, I found myself lost in the painted room screens, their gardens filled with hyacinths and tea roses and weeping willows and pigeons. I rested my gilded teacup upon a knee-high table and imagined myself in their landscape, languidly strolling among the flowers and trees on the zigzag path. There would have been nothing to occupy me but to observe the spread of the vegetation, the rise of tree trunks, and the blossoming of enormous flowers. But I soon found myself bored and restless there. My fingers dipped into a rushing stream. However, there were no challenges, or learning of scientific facts, or patients needing me, patients and doctors to be contended with. There was not enough to do. I had helped Mrs. Thompson. I suspected she was past danger and would, most likely, live.

I stopped my daydreaming and turned toward Mary, who was dusting a bronze planter with an abundant plant reaching out from its depths toward her. Her hair was a gathering storm, the cross was tucked beneath the neck of her gray dress. "Where was James last night?"

"I do not know, Miss."

But even if she did know she would not tell me. I was not a Thompson and privileged to that sort of information. If James had wanted me to know he would have told me. But I was not privileged to any carryings-on about the house that I did not observe myself. "You must be tired, Mary."

"Yes, Miss. But my mistress is improving with our prayers and attention. I'm trying to keep on with my other duties."

I placed my teacup upon the table that was the same height as Fu and saw my wound curving along, paralleling, the rim of the cup. It moved as my hand moved, creating new designs upon my hand. "I shall go to the hospital today as they need me there as well."

"I shall send for you if Mrs. Thompson needs you." And she resumed her nervous dusting, cleaning to fill the time, a knitting of the tense air, until she was called to Mrs. Thompson's bedside again.

~

I was stranded by the apothecary cabinet at the hospital, lingering a little too long at the bootsole-shaped colours refracted through the glass bottles and then the glass doors. I was weary and liked their bleariness, lack of edges, and lack of motion. I felt much kinship with them. I did not recognize their precise colours and the fact that they must be shifting incrementally with the sun. Mabel caught me staring at the wall. She placed a jar of powdered rhubarb that looked to be all aflame upon a shelf. She clucked with her mouth.

"And there being so much to do round here." She sucked in the thin ridge of her lips, her spidery fingers released the jar, settling onto the sharp corner of the cabinet.

"Ah, but there is stillness here in this room that is lovely, that I cannot find at the Thompson house. And I am weary from attending to Mrs. Thompson last night."

"Is she improving?"

"Yes, I believe she shall recover."

"And my rooms are too quiet, except for the early morning fishmongers. You need to visit sometime. The rooms are too empty."

"But I am pleased that you are making it on your own, Mabel."

"Without any drink. With the job here. I'm getting by." She tufted some rags between her bony fingers. "Better than being at Elizabeth's." She made a sour face. "Too many hands there doing all sorts a things, and worries about where I'd end up." She pushed the rags aside. "When I'm working here I'm busy and forgetting my worries."

"You appear to be a good nurse."

"I'm still learning and Dr. Lawrence said I could be learning from you."

I began to wonder what she could learn from me—was I a killer or merely kind? Was I a good nurse or simply sympathetic? A scientist or someone who stitched various theories together to attempt to make a whole philosophy?

I could hear a patient moaning beneath the distorted print of the Madonna. I had been shocked at how the Madonna's lovely face had dampened and pulled downward from the leaks. One touch and I knew she would fall out of her frame in dirty, rough pieces. She resembled Mrs. Tatterspol before she died, one side of her washing away. I wanted to bandage her, cover her crisscrossing scars, the flesh that gathered too much in one place. I could still make out her face like a length of cloth I was to cut and sew into a skirt, the pattern emerging. Her baby was squeezed to nothing at her side, barely visible. The paper bulged from the frame as if growing muscles. And I could feel it—the body hinged, thick and thin, and dissolving into softness. It hurt. That pull toward nothing. That tender disintegration into a pool of soggy paper. The red dress bled over the frame, leaving a space behind the wall. It had begun to turn brown.

Mabel noticed that I was staring at the old engraving too long. "Dirty old thing." And she went to it and took it down from the wall. The print collapsed in pieces upon itself and became two handfuls of paper. She wrapped it in rags to be disposed of. "Now show me how to mix up laudanum."

And I did, taking the fine red powder and letting it vein through the clear liquid. Showing her the proportions, thinking of fine, blossoming flowers. I taught her how to bandage stumps and fix the pillows. How to patch a strong poultice. And more. I wanted to teach her all that I knew and she proved to be a quick learner. But when I showed her how to hold a patient's hand after a surgery or procedure, she balked.

"I ain't holding their dirty parts for nothing." She turned away. "I'd rather hold Sam or Betts or Lily if'n they were still alive."

"You are doing very well without the comfort."

"I'll leave that part to ye." And she left the ward.

Before I crept down the stairs toward the kitchen I sat in a chair near the window at the back for a bit of fresh air. I strained to hear the horses, the clap of their hooves upon the street nearby. The men were swearing and talking as they set up their carts. I could imagine the vegetables all laid out, the meat, and fish with their dead eyes, the sweets and the lush flowers jostling for attention. I could almost see the horses all thin and bent from their work, the warm, sweet breath along my arm as I reached to stroke one. The way his mouth would chew upon his bit and he could lean toward my hand without looking at me as I touched his rough hair, his flank shivering as if I were a fly. His large, dark eye could look ahead of him as his nostrils snorted at times. The stamp of his feet. It was all I could hear. At that tired moment I believed it would not have been so awful to be a leisurely woman with not much more to do than to spend time with the horses. They were a diversion, even though one that had gone astray or reared for a moment had irreparably harmed Mrs. Thompson.

Dr. Lawrence rushed by, peering down at my hand. "I see you are well, Miss Russell. I am glad." He stopped for a moment and his beard swayed to the side. "I am pleased that there was no infection." He traced the slit that would become a scar along my hand. "Good to see you back," and he left before I could say anything.

I nervously made my way down the stairs as if I were afraid a giant rat or another version of Mabel would harm me. I supposed it was memories and I was being inconsistent, as I was about many small things. I slipped one foot after another down the steps. In my mind I composed a small poem, "Imperceptible, the patter of tiny feet/ that once had rocked the floor,/ now only a silence issues forth/ that had not been exorcised before." An eerie quiet attended my echoing footsteps. It was dark and damp and there was no activity except for the clatter of teapots and plates in the kitchen. The odour of a strong, earthy tea was steeping and its steam was coiling up into the air. I stood before the kitchen and turned around and around as though I were dancing, for there was too much space and too much silence. I thought of how empty Mabel must have felt with her excessive humanness, the silly hands and feet, the lack of tails or feathers or claws. How we attempted to conquer all that surrounded us.

I could have written down my little poem, called it "Rats." Perhaps I would. I did miss writing Flo letters, gathering my thoughts, my emotions greeted and gathered, to be labeled and placed into medicine jars. It was a task I had rarely done before and was discouraged in entertaining in my family home. My sister would push my pen onto the table, order me to play with her or else she would tell our mother that I had been melancholy and distracted again. I was warned that I might need another water cure at Umberslade. When we were older my mother needed me to stay imprisoned in the drawing room with her and my sister.

And then there was writing to Flo. Flo? And I suddenly remembered my appointment with her with a start. I had been distracted by Mrs. Thompson's accident and my own small one. It was so important and yet somehow frightening. It was in an hour and I had forgotten. My mind was too filled with nooks and crannies. My face turned the colour of claret and I ran up the stairs and through the ward, saying to both Dr. Lawrence and Mabel, who were leaning over a patient in bed,

"I must run. I have a previous appointment." The exhaustion that coursed through my body was held at bay willy-nilly and my overwrought mouth opened wide and gulped air.

~

I stopped once to use a window as a looking-glass before I hurriedly arrived at Flo's doorstep. I saw the same long, oval face I had always met when I cared to look. I straightened my hair, pulled at my high collar, and adjusted my skirt. My dark eyes stared and I felt as though a hand missing two fingers helped to soothe me, touching my cheek. I tidied myself up as best I could. At her doorstep I applied more lavender scent, although Flo would, mostly likely, not object to the hospital odour.

I entered 35 South Street, near Hyde Park. I was greeted by Flo's maid, who wore a freshly starched apron; her shoes clicked along the floors as she led me to the ground floor sitting room. She was spotted with freckles that dusted her entire face, including her eyelids. She had a stern, plain face.

The room was simple, with a dark floral rug; her numerous bookcases overflowed with reports, opened books, government blue books. There were sturdy tables and chairs cut from a pale brown wood nearly the colour of flesh. There was an engraving of the ceiling at the Sistine Chapel upon the wall. The maid offered me a pen, ink and stationary to clearly describe my business with Flo. I wrote, "I am your friend, Ann Russell, here to visit you as we had arranged."

The maid took the note saying, "She is feeling weak today and rather unfit. It may be quite impossible to see her today."

I could not read the maid's eyes, wondering whether Flo

would see me. I rested my hand upon my sleeve but my heart loudly pushed against my skin and reverberated, drumming against my forehead also. The moment lengthened and I was uncomfortable wondering how much I meant to her. The ceiling of the Sistine Chapel fell down toward me as my eyes caught on the engraving. It tumbled in all its beauty. Upstairs lay Flo, another sleeping beauty of sorts, although she would not consider herself as such. Illness had tethered her to bed. It was a pity that she was so unwell after all the soldiers and patients she had helped. My heart swirled in my chest and then calmed like a current that had finally been tamed. And the maid turned and went up the stairs. I listened to her footsteps until I could not hear them anymore. There was a soft murmur of voices but I could not hear much. Then the sound of her shoes as she descended was a scraping like a saw awful on bones.

"Miss Nightingale has not slept in several days and has spent the last few nights reading books and taking notes. She wrote many letters and answered much correspondence and is very weak."

I could feel her breath. Her lips tightened. I envied her proximity to Flo. Hera reached up and slapped me with a ghostly wing. The owl was trying to tell me that the past was always with us. I wanted to respond that I understood but that it was always a one-sided conversation with the dead. I expected the maid to turn me away and end my precious visit with Flo. It was then that I imagined the maid dead. No more breathing, the stiff, thin lips permanently fixed in a closed position. She was caught and still as she began to walk away, the shape of her body stopped, the legs and arms frozen just so. I hated her for possibly turning me away from Flo. I pushed the thought from my mind just as she opened her mouth, continued.

"But she says that she will see you now, for only a brief while."

And as we ascended the stairs together I thought of the maid's skirts as yellow flowers, blooming during the day, waving about her legs as she walked in their slight breeze. I remembered playing with Rose when we were young children and how we had lined up all our dolls upon a rug. They were all deceased one afternoon. This was before Rose caught the fever that killed her, when her long, blonde hair was tucked into the backs of her knees as she kneeled down, adjusting a lifeless arm just so. A youthful Mrs. Thompson stopped in the bedchamber and with her large, plump face said, "Playing again? Good girls." We laughed heartily when she closed the bedchamber door and we jerked the doll bodies about, had their eyes roll back, their mouths too dry to speak.

"This was how my doggie died," Rose said, as fascinated with death as I was. "Now they have no more pain. That's what my mommy said."

James caught us bathing a doll and when I told him that they did not have any more pain he began calling me "Pain" as though I could inflict or remove pain or that I was frivolous enough to try. I did not see Rose after she caught the fever. I knew it could have easily been me who caught it. I thought of her tongue swollen, her eyes too wide, all that beautiful hair cut away from her damp forehead and head. Her childish delirium. Now I did not have to imagine it, having seen it too many times.

My heart fluttered and rose in my chest as we went into the bedchamber where cut flowers gestured from her bedside table. I had heard that Lady Ashburton and other admirers sent her flowers weekly. The white walls appeared whiter as sunlight flooded in, without curtains or sashes. A small pear tree peered through her window, unencumbered. The branches were filled with thick leaves and the start of small fruit. A fireplace faced the bed; a bookcase stood sentry behind her headboard with two lamps. On the mantle was a chromolithograph that said, "It is I. Be not Afraid," her initial call from her God. Between two windows Flo sat uncomfortably in her chaise lounge upon which a design of buds and flowers grew. Pictures of Sebastopol lined the walls and I felt suddenly at home again. Was I too old to admire someone so much? Yet I knew I was not alone, there was a whole nation. A pile of letters sat flibberty-gibbet upon a table. Some had fallen to the floor and scattered, like large, white footprints.

I saw immediately that Flo's round, kind face had grown older, as had mine. She wore a Buckinghamshire lace headscarf tied around her head, with eyelets of lace that matched her sleeve cuffs. She was bathed in light from the windows; sunlight tapped her thick knuckles and experienced fingers and then it fled. She held a shifting stack of letters upon her lap, above a blanket. She was wearing two shawls, one folded upon the other, although the day was warm for Springtime. When her face lifted to mine I was transported back to the noisy barracks, to the sick soldiers, well over ten years ago. The floral pattern of the chaise lounge appeared too busy for her calm, unhurried visage.

"She has but a few moments to receive you as she needs her strength for her work," the maid cautioned and then left, her shoes making an ugly music on the stairs.

I sat by Flo upon a plain but comfortable sage green chair. Her face twisted toward me like a chrysanthemum rising toward sunlight. Her eyes alighted upon my hand. She took it into hers, rotated it, and carefully examined the scar that was forming. My skin upon her skin felt electric. It was an attraction and a jolt throughout my body, although Flo did not appear to feel anything out of the ordinary. The hair along my arms stood upright beneath the sleeves of my dress and I almost pulled my hand away as the sensation was overwhelming. Then she returned my hand.

"Did you not have fever with this wound?"

"No, I was glad I did not. We keep the ward at the hospital well ventilated and clean." I peered at my hand. "A doctor was handing me an instrument and I was cut."

"The doctors must learn to be more careful. Did you bleed much?"

"Yes, somewhat. But enough about my unfortunate accident. How are you feeling, Flo?"

"It is good that you are able to work. I still believe that I will live and die in hospital. I had thought of St. Thomas's. I am weak today, with a spasm of the heart this morning. I must be carried from room to room as I cannot bear my own weight. Some days I cannot move at all."

"I am so sorry to hear that."

"I have used injections of opium but they cloud my thoughts and I do not want to be unfit for my correspondence and notes and reports." She smiled wanly. "I remember you as a good nurse, Ann Russell, working hard for our children in the Crimea. It is easy to get carried away with the war and forget proprieties, to want to forget where you are, to desire to forget what you are doing. I also remember you said you did not want to submit to the nurses' caps as they were uncomfortable and did not suit all faces."

I smiled.

She continued, "I remember when you helped a surgeon perform an operation on a young soldier's sternum and the blood flew into the air and shocked us all."

"Now there is little that shocks me about the body." I shifted in my chair. "And I certainly do not fuss over a nurse's cap."

We both laughed although Flo's laugh was shallow, short, and quiet, obviously quite painful.

"I have been privileged of late to your thoughts by letter," she said. "Although I cannot respond quickly, be certain that I have read them all." She closed her eyes. "You have had a difficult time. How is Mrs. Thompson?"

"It is all God's will now." I could see how frail she was, so unlike the physically active Flo in the Crimea, but she still had her spirit. "I have heard from my God and He has guided me."

Her eyes brightened. "I was just writing Julius Mohl about theodicy—the belief that evil is necessary for great good and that both are balanced out upon the world. And about the Sufis. The discussion concerns whether their God is considered as good or evil by us or is somewhere in between."

"I do not know much about theology, only that I heard His voice."

"Yes," she said wincing, "I, too, received several calls from God. I remember my first one on a rough wooden bench under two enormous Cedars of Lebanon at Embley, my family's home near Hampshire. That was in 1837. I worked as hard as I could among the poor people after that. I was told about a quest and that at its end a secret would be revealed." She smiled thinly, "Perhaps the quest was the Crimean War and the secret was my unknowing part in the death of so many of the soldiers there."

"Yes," I said. "I remember much of the war, perhaps too much of it."

"Is there such a thing? For do we not want to learn from what we saw and did?"

"Perhaps," I ventured. I thought of her illness. I waited and continued, "Once I saw you alone tending to two dying soldiers in the corner room of the barracks." My heart leapt in remembrance.

Her watery, gray eyes alighted upon a chair arm. "You viewed me severing their arteries?"

Our eyes met, hers caught upon mine. "Yes, it was swift and painless."

"I had not been aware of anyone there."

"I was just then rounding a corner with a bowl of entrails from an operation and I had wanted to ask you a question. I was quiet and left." It was then that I had understood, had discovered love.

"Oh," and her eyes fluttered. "The incident is not to be repeated to anyone as you must well know since you have not as yet."

"I shall keep your secret." I lifted her hand and kissed it. For I had secrets of my own that, perhaps, one day I could share with her.

"They were in such pain, their bodies so mangled by the war."

"Yes." And I kissed her hand again. She recoiled in pain and moved a leg underneath a blanket. I wanted to crawl beneath Flo's blanket and comfort her. "It was a kindness."

Her sweet, round face troubled the wall and came back to me. "I do not have those inclinations." And she removed her hand.

Perhaps I had been kissing her hand too much. "Yes, I knew that in the Crimea. I am terribly sorry."

"Yes, the kiss there. We shall forget it. But I may need a strong nurse in the future for my own health and to help with reports to the India Sanitary Commission."

"I hope you will consider me." For if anyone could understand me, Flo could. I loved her. Not merely her reputation but I loved her failing body, a sacrifice to the war, and her curious, lively mind. I intertwined my hands upon my lap, for they could be disobedient.

"Have you been abroad?"

"No, not since the Crimea."

She sighed. "It helps in understanding the health problems of the colonies and the other countries." She took my hand. "You are one of my favorite nurses and still quite strong. I can see that." Her tired head sank into the flowered chaise lounge.

"Yes." I was elated. I squeezed her hand without thinking and she winced. "Do you believe that by ending suffering we are stealing anyone's life?"

Her eyes flew up to mine. "We each have our own lives, no matter how short or wretched they are." She closed her eyes. "It is up to each person how they want to spend theirs."

I could see that she was tired. "I will see my own way out."

"Yes, I have much work to do."

"I have Mrs. Thompson and the hospital to attend to." I was at the door.

"Do not rub your sores, Ann." Her voice was fading, growing softer, disappearing.

But I was not certain what she meant.

Leaving

I found Mrs. Thompson without her bonnet but still in her bedclothes beneath her covers, and she was no longer sleeping or delirious, as I had feared. Her once white bonnet with some yellow stains had been thrown to the bottom of her bed where her Chinese dog peered at me between his paws, following me with his eyes. He was resting comfortably in the area where her leg had been and was no longer. He did not bark or run about in circles as I entered the room, as though he were only concerned about his mistress and did not want to disturb her. Mary was leaving the room with a chamber pot that sloshed as she carried it.

"Mary, be careful with that. I do not want any spilled upon the floor," Mrs. Thompson cautioned and I was pleased to know that she was well again. Mary's boots kicked up from behind her skirt as she was nearly out the door. "And I want my bonnet cleaned also." But Mary did not appear to hear her as she continued out the door.

It was now twilight, before any candles or lamps were lit, and I felt as though I were floating, as I had not yet slept enough. Silence surrounded us like smoke from a flame. We were each lost in our own thoughts. It was that time of evening when all the textures molded into one, a silken garment became the same as coarse hessian, or a leaf the same as the rough skin of wood. A piece of paper was no different in texture to the window glass tangled with branches just outside its reach. It was the details that failed to exist. Like certain memories that tended to fade. Some days all the Crimean soldiers' faces merged into one. When I was tired. They all became Martin Farland, with his mustache and the curling, dark hair framing the landscape of his forehead. His long nose below the meadow of his hair, his uniform with its high-necked jacket. It was always the uniform that rose clearly in my mind. Not the faces. Those I shunned.

I turned to Mrs. Thompson. "I am glad that you are becoming well. May I do something to make you more comfortable?" For now there were just the two of us in the room.

"James left this morning. And before he left we discussed the nature of grief. He said it was loss, a leg, children, one's husband or father. To me, grief was reaching out and having no one left there but my tiny Fu. It was being left with only a memory. I said it was a shock to one's system and way of life. I would give anything to get out of bed and dress myself or go out or to simply play with my dog." She stopped for a moment. "Grief is looking out of the window glass and everything appearing so very far away and unattainable."

Again it was the fuzzy details. The things that one forgot or took for granted in one's day that could no longer be had. I sat by her bedside. "That, in time, will pass. I shall teach you to move about when you are fully healed."

"It is difficult to hold onto what you love. Remember that, Ann."

I could not tell her that that was something I already knew and had already lost. "You still have James." Although I knew he was often busy.

"He claims that we are losing all our money from investments by my late husband. That Mr. Thompson had kept the knowledge from us. And that I have made it worse by listening to Mrs. Tatterspol."

She had become uncharacteristically philosophical and worrisome since her accident. I was concerned for her well being.

"I am so alone," she said. "And I cannot walk about. And if we are to be poor..." and she did not finish her statement. Instead she tidied the covers. "I miss Mrs. Tatterspol also."

"I know there are so many people to miss."

"You have been kind to me, Ann. You have tended to me well and often. I cannot describe that horrible accident. The horse reared for no reason and the hooves came down upon me, the carriage leaped ahead and then I was somehow beneath it. I do not remember much."

"Try not to concern yourself with the memory. It is sufficient for now that your mind has returned to us. It is a good thing."

"Good for whom?"

"Good for your recovery, of course."

"I do not know if I want to recover." Her plump face had thinned already and the angles of bones were becoming more visible.

"Why not?" I sensed she had thought about this. I was growing annoyed. But Mrs. Thompson continued.

"I always thought that a person went on or they did not. I had forgotten about the in-between. Until Mrs. Tatterspol. I thought that they either lived or died." She playfully poked her Chinese dog with a finger. "Now which one am I? I am not certain I want to continue living, to go on like this." She said it nonchalantly, not caring. Not like the others that were suffering, but as though she was choosing a dress for some occasion, just another choice. "You do not believe me, Ann, do you?"

"I think you will heal from this in time." I could not take her seriously. I did not want to.

"Then you do not know me very well. For I mean what I say."

I wondered whether she would be sullen, but she was not. I was quiet.

"I wish to die and you must consider my request earnestly. Or at least allow me my choice through the laudanum you have given me. I have heard of people doing so before. A nurse can leave it by my bedside, thereupon, I can drink it myself. It is not much to ask for." She paused. "You have cared for me for some time now."

"Yes, but you have been through other illnesses and I believe you are made of sterner stuff." I found myself arguing with her. I had never done so before with other patients. I was emotionally exhausted, whereas previously I had only felt exhilarated after making patients happy. I did not want to decide. Since Mrs. Thompson felt every nick and cut acutely, should I listen to her entreaties? Or ignore them? Did how I felt about her sway my decision? What if James found out? Did it matter that it had been an accident? Could Mrs. Thompson regain her full life and health and regret her decision? Was that my concern? It had not been so difficult at the barracks. Then it had been less complicated. I had not known the others. Now I knew my patient too well.

Meanwhile Mrs. Thompson had tilted her head towards the window and began sobbing in great bursts. Her dog became excited and ran about, leaping from side to side over her bosom. "I am not made of such stern stuff," she blubbered. "I do miss my husband and I do wish to meet him soon."

I sighed as Mary entered the room with a clean chamber pot. Mrs. Thompson continued crying but more softly now.

"There, there, Mrs. Thompson," Mary said, depositing the chamber pot, and taking her hand. "It will all be over soon." She did not think about what she said; only that she was comforting her.

I noticed then that the room had grown dark. It swallowed each of us, the way shadows made knives innocuous, no longer shiny or sharp looking. The darkness made me feel sad and silent, cheated of distractions that would take my mind from Flo and Mrs. Thompson. The long night stretched ahead of me. I wanted to sleep but now could not. Mrs. Thompson asked too much of me. It appeared overwhelming, terrible. All I wanted was a cup of tea, a bath with cans of hot water from the kitchen, and then sleep. An oblivion that I, too, recognized and desired but would eventually wake from. Was she relinquishing all too easily?

I touched the cold glass of the window and shivered as I tried to find a candle. Would Hera spread out her wings again? Would Sleeping Beauty ever awaken? The dog had calmed and so had Mrs. Thompson. Mary sat by her side also. Darkness closed about me tightly and I could no longer see the floorboards or the curtains. Cut flowers might be watching me and I would not know it. I could not see the knots, the scars, and gouges, the blood, the empty shoes. Sometimes I did not mind the darkness and it made the room seem nearly empty, when all was quiet and peaceful. The air grew cooler and I lit a candle, which cast twisting and troubled shadows like witches' spells upon all of us. The little dog appeared to grow large and

black and trembled, escaping along the wall. A glass upon the
table seemed almost human, dancing or clamouring for attention. It seemed we could not hold our shapes in the dark. I had
thought that Flo could not see who had kissed her in the dark
in the Crimea. But she had. Just as I had seen her with the two
soldiers. I resolved to prove myself a worthy nurse to Flo and it
would not help if I killed Mrs. Thompson.

Mary and I lit candles and lamps and the room changed,
becoming warm and cozy. All returned from hiding. The sharp
smell of burnt hair permeated the room as Mary had bent too
low to a flame that had caught and consumed several strands
and was immediately extinguished. We would have laughed
had it been another time.

Mrs. Thompson's expressionless face wound in and out of
the shadows. I recalled that she was better at giving orders than
asking favors, and that if she had her way, I would bend to her
desires. As it was, I obeyed everyone else's requests, the doctors, the patients, my family's, and my God's. I was tired. The
window was blind, became reflective. I saw our three, torn figures rising and falling in the glass. I slid into a chair, could feel
its stiff, wooden shoulder against my own. The thick stuffing
at the center embraced me and I sank deeper into it. I watched
Mary circle about Mrs. Thompson like her Chinese dog. I
thought, now why cannot Mary do it? I was distraught and yet
my eyes flickered open and then shut. Soon I was dreaming.

~

Mabel and I ascended with her belongings from the hospital cellar. Two crates, a scarred, wooden chair, rag-tag blankets
with tiny chew holes scattered like freckles along the edges.

We blew upon these objects and white powder flew into the air. Rat dust. We did not find any small skeletons strewn about but we did see the evidence of their gnawing. In my peripheral vision I did notice something scurrying once in that profusion of darkness but I did not mention it to Mabel. I was curious to view the remnants of Mabel's former life, the clues to her past, the talisman of her future.

"Eh, you ain't going to find anything a value in here," she said, dragging a box to the entrance of the ward.

"I am aware of that, but we should clean it up, as Dr. Lawrence requested."

Dr. Lawrence passed us as he talked with a colleague. He rubbed his waving beard as though he heard me mention his name.

But I eagerly opened the crate I had carried up the stairs. It was lightweight and when I pried off the top, dried nests made of bits of mattresses, stuffing, rags, paper, and two blackened, bent spoons caught my eye. Then three cracked and chipped plates from the kitchen, different-sized rusty nails, pieces of glass arranged by colour, a comb made of bone that was yellowing and missing several prongs. I lifted the comb and turned it over and over in my palm, held it out, and wrinkled my nose.

"Ye'd never make it in the frontier, my dear, or upon the London streets."

She was actually very clever to have lived in the hospital, however long she lived there, a few years, I had heard. For it had sources of food, water, and other necessary stuffs for surviving. "How did you choose what to keep, Mabel?" I replaced the comb and lifted an intricate nest that had a green, frayed ribbon woven about its circumference. I wondered how other people made choices.

"This was all I had." She smiled. "I don need it anymore. I have me own rooms filled with wonderful things."

"Such as?"

"A new chair and nice plates. Come and see it, dearie."

"Perhaps someday I will." Mabel had a whole new life. I walked to the other box. "What is in this one?"

We did not have many patients at the time but one moaned and Mabel left to tend to him before she answered. I carefully lifted the lid of the box and found an odd collection of shoes. When I took some out I discovered that they were both men's and women's and that, most often, I could not find a companion, but only one right or left shoe.

Dr. Lawrence quietly approached me as I stood just outside of the ward. He tapped my shoulder, startling me. "I am sorry to tell you that a messenger came to say that Mrs. Thompson has died." And he proceeded to discuss the complications from an operation such as she had, how the blood often poisons the body. But I was merely half-listening and nodding my head, thinking how I had just left her sleeping peacefully but two hours ago. I woke up this morning to find myself still in the chair across from her bed. She was sleeping quietly with the dog nestled beneath one arm. Or was she sleeping? Had I released Mrs. Thompson while sleepwalking? While dreaming? Perhaps Mary had done it when I was not looking? Or perhaps while I watched them. Her fever could have returned with dire complications. Or could it have been James? I supposed I would never know. Hopefully her daughter Rose, her husband, and Mrs. Tatterspol had finally come to collect her. That left James alone and I had not seen him for a while.

I had tiptoed out of Mrs. Thompson's bedchamber this morning, washed quickly, then dressed and gone to the hospital. She had not stirred when I left although I saw the little dog peek at me and then his head fell again upon his paw. Nothing to worry about, he seemed to say.

After Dr. Lawrence went on his way, I quickly left the hospital without saying a word. Dr. Lawrence was not surprised to see me leave. The flowers and bushes and trees in the garden outside rushed toward me as I passed them. Their perfume reached me just as I swept by them. When I looked back at the hospital, for a moment, I thought I saw Mabel at a hospital window. I did not wave, but walked on.

~

A bright slash of late afternoon light rested upon Mrs. Thompson's empty pillow. As I passed by her bedchamber I thought of her bonnet perched upon her head and how she did not survive all her losses. The door was ajar and loneliness and silence pervaded the house. I could not hear Mary or anyone else about. I was completely alone. In my room, I sat at Rose's desk and knew I would need to leave now that Mrs. Thompson was gone. I dreaded my family house with my mother and sister. The fence of my spine rested against the small chair. I took up my pen, dipped it, then held it resting upon the knuckle above my wound's scar, my seam, my white stitch.

*My Dearest,*

*It was delightful to see you although you were feeling so poorly. I was grateful for the visit and the opportunity to speak to you.*

*As you may have heard, Mrs. Thompson was called home suddenly. Her leg was recently amputated, the result of an injury from a horse. I assisted the surgeon, but there were complications. Mrs. Thompson had expressed a desire to leave this world and in that, her wish had been granted.*

## Up and Away

The night before Mrs. Thompson's funeral I had instructed Mary to press the black mourning garments I had kept folded in the bottom of my travelling trunk. I had so hoped that I would not have to use them. In the morning, after I had employed the washstand and dressed, the blackness was a curtain about my body. The scar on my hand was a splinter of white against my dark clothes. James knocked upon my door. Sheets of my clothing rippled as I went to the door, although my overskirt had been tied back into a train by Mary, who lingered in the room. I wore an elaborate bonnet, chosen beforehand by my mother who anticipated these types of situations.

James wore suitable black men's attire, and even Mary wore mourning clothes. As Mary had dressed me that morning I had commented that Mrs. Thompson had died suddenly after doing so well beforehand.

"That's the way of it sometimes," she said buttoning my dress.

"I believe it had been her wish to prepare for the Presence of God."

"Had it been, Miss?"

But I did not answer her, for I was turning this way and that and lifting my arms for her. And our conversation faded, muffled by masses of black clothing.

James led us to the parlour where a fire warmed the cool
early summer night. Firelight filled the cracks and holes in all
the equipment that attempted to contain it. James and I sat at
opposite ends of the fire while Mary stood by the door, her
breath wheezy.

"How is your work with electricity and electromagnetism
progressing?"

"I am sorry to say that I have all but abandoned it lately–
with my obligations to Mother." He laced his fingers together.
"I must speak to you..."

I interrupted him, "I am readying myself to leave and I am
filling my travelling trunk. I will return to my family home
very shortly."

He sat back, relaxed. "You may have heard that I have financial problems. But I wish you the best of luck and was glad
for this time together for now I cannot help but think of us as
close as brother and sister."

"What will you do?"

"I wish to become a scientist."

"Yes," I said. "Of course."

~

Mabel's rooms were near Hampstead, near where I had
spied her that day with the sort-of-gentleman. Past the Flask
tavern and Well Walk, where, over a century ago, spa water the colour of iron was poured into flasks and sold for its
health benefits. Past Keat's house and Jack Straw's Castle. Well
past them. The rooms were off a cobbled street where people,
mostly women and children, were shouting or hovered about
their doorsteps or dangled their limbs out of a window. We

walked straight into her parlour as there was not a hall or other room to pass through and it was peculiar in that there was the chair and dishes Mabel had mentioned, but very little else. A disturbing sketch of a nude was the only decoration upon her walls.

"I found this one," she tapped the picture. "Found it on the street in an alley. Pretty thing, ain't it?"

"Yes," I said, looking closer, seeing the lines were drawn in brownish ink or perhaps animal blood. It was a wild, abstracted thing, the model being too thin and having too many angles. The perspective and shadows did not seem accurate.

Mabel fetched her water from a pump several houses down and she asked me if I wanted tea.

"Not just now, thank you." But I was impressed with her offer and her effort.

It was thankfully clean in the large kitchen with a wooden floor. There were several large rooms, each with old, white, iron bedsteads whose paint flaked into piles of snow upon the floor. There was no other furniture. She did, however, share a washhouse and privy with the other tenants of the building, one older woman and a gnarled, older man. She did not have curtains, so the sunlight blared in the room. It was simple and practical, like Mabel.

"It ain't really finished yet here." She turned and winked at me. "It's waiting for you to move in and fix it up. I could spare the room and could do with the money."

"I must think about it." I knew I would think about her offer longer and more often than she had thought about decorating her rooms.

"We could work together." She looked at the empty walls and I noticed a spreading claw of dampness staining a corner.

All the imperfections were so visible without ornamentation. The walls needed pictures to hide their cracks and stains. "It's nice living on yer own. No mistress or family or husband telling ya what to do."

"Yes," and it burst out of me unrehearsed. "I will stay here temporarily until I find other lodgings."

"Good," she said. The back of her brown dress was shapeless; her hair was tightly wound into a knot. "You can move in anytime. Did you like what decoration I've learned from Elizabeth?" She waved her arms at the walls and made a sour face, her mouth chewing upon itself.

"Where did you grow up, Mabel?"

"Here and there."

But I knew she must have grown up somewhere and I would have time to discover where. Soon enough.

"Do you like nursing?"

"There's always a reason why a person helps another person—it can be an excuse so they feel better, or to get something."

Hers was a gloomy view of humanity, but I could not blame her. "Perhaps I will get another owl," I said to the new Mabel whose fingernails were bitten down into half moons, who could still look wicked in the half light, but who possessed more independence and self-reliance than I had once imagined.

"Maybe you will," she said to me, someone who would learn to carry a coal scuttle up some stairs and water in a pail from a community pump. And I wanted to learn.

I imagined my travel books in a spare room, piled and waiting for me. I peered out a curtainless window. A hot air balloon was rising from a park past the tops of the houses. All nearby heads were turned in it's direction. Probably a wedding, I thought, as a distant white figure in the wicker basket waved a gloved hand. I envisioned it going to Greece, Egypt, India. New places with new ideas. Different lives entirely.

Part IV

Abyssinia, 1868


I cannot help what I do. I am standing in a field of fallen
men. Some are waving their brown arms or parts of arms at
me and begging for my help. Blood flows from their gaping
wounds, their mouths are perpetually screaming. It is a small
battle compared to the Crimea, here on the Arogi plateau. Their
skin is a pile of dry leaves shivering at my feet. Richard Wellfield is here, somewhere, with the 4th King's Own regiment. I
have lost sight of his blood-splattered helmet, his own Snider
rifle with my flowered ribbon tied to its barrel. The muskets
and spears of the Abyssinian forces lie scattered among the
men and body parts, resembling abandoned toys. Rockets still
shatter the air. Brown hills rise up in the distance like too much
flesh, the sky is dry and clear. The smell of burning powder
and blood collide, thwart one another. Sky is erased above the
men's continual crying. It is another language. But I still understand it. It has taken us nearly three months to reach here from
India. We had crossed scrublands, plains, and farms before the
hills and mountains rose up, reached for us. So we could arrive
at the fortress of Magdala.


~


In London I had kept Richard's card and rubbed it between

my fingertips until it grew soft from my touching it. When *The London Times* printed an article on how King Theodore II of Abyssinia held Captain Cameron, along with several British women and children, as hostages, I knew I had to depart. Apparently the king had not had a response from Queen Victoria for help concerning warfare with his Moslem neighbors after he had tried to contact her several times. I found Richard in a clean boarding house and discussed the matter with him and he was delighted.

"We must leave tomorrow," he said. "They shall need us."

"Fine," I said. I had left my trunks in a pile at Mabel's but had not as yet unpacked them. I closed my eyes and believed that my life was an approximation of war, that death had always been a tree rinsed with light that I could fall into, that would hold me. My own acts of heresy were personal and I held them close to me. I could breath death's fragrance, distinct, intricate, something swallowed, something that lingered, newly created each time.

Sir Robert Napier led us through mountains where strange new animals leaped and crawled and flew, a musical muzzle, human fingers, threadbare eyes, skin the colour of mangoes, thin veils covering snouts, orange tails, a body shaped like a pear, snow-like paws, a church-bell cry, feathers that resembled claws and spears, fur with mustard-green stains, eyes that reflected the landscape around them. It rained suddenly, drenching us, and then stopped. Villagers watched us like tigers, trailing us, hunting us, staring at us from the lace of any vegetation, from behind boulders. They ran from side to side in their colourful attire, their bare limbs. Sometimes we heard the swish of a skirt or the clicking of jewelry, reminding me of Mrs. Tatterspol in my old life. I could feel their eyes, the lilt of a tongue pondering our destination. Then they vanished. There were several other nurses and one doctor, but I did not talk to them at length. We did the best we could, following the men. Richard Wellfield was solicitous, yet occupied with the preparations for war.

"It is good to have returned to help the empire, is it not, Miss Russell?" His red whiskers were now unruly, his dust-coloured hair greasy and dark and long. His hand, empty of two fingers, was reportedly still quite handy with a rifle. His green striped eyes glowed. His sad mouth now appeared to pantomime happiness.

"Yes, indeed, it is good, Richard Wellfield." I cautiously smiled. I, too, was happy.

~

Blood slides from a man's mouth as he is trying to speak, to say words I cannot understand. His hands are trembling. I believe he is calling for a nurse in his own language. I bend down, take his awkward hand. He closes his singed eyelids, lids that are blackened like fruit left outside too long. A British soldier stumbles by, his breeches brown with dirt and old blood, and shoots the man in the head with his Snider. The injured man's hand falls from mine and his body curls into the dry soil, his eyes half open. It has happened so quickly that I am not shocked. I linger, thinking how this man appears smaller in death than he did in life a moment ago. Without gestures and speech and breath in the space between us, he is hardly there anymore. He is already drier, unmoving, lost like a discarded shirt or pair of trousers, containing what? What is left of the body? And for a moment I want to exchange my life for his, his death unexpectedly unbearable, having cared for him for but a fraction of his life. And then I am filled with a sudden joy that I am still alive.

I drag three wounded men into my nurse's tent. They are a fraction of the wounded and I am overwhelmed. I am wet with blood and water from a short, tropical rain, like the monsoon rains we had in India. Mud coats my hands and wrists and ankles, drying soon, tumbling off in pieces, small, fat lumps of brown flour that I step upon and they crumble back into the soil. I work upon the three men. One dies quickly. Another's side is crushed by a shell and he cries out, tossing. The third injured one was shot twice in the chest and he clutches my hand and spouts much gibberish that I translate as either *thank you* or *please let me die*. Then he falls silent. I bandage one and stop the seeping blood of the other.

The battle is over in nearly two hours and all is quiet but for the moans and shouts of men. Straw from the men's beds crunches underfoot. Puffs of brown hills surround the tent like exhalations. It is beginning to grow darker and I could discern the various shades of brown in the horizon, on the mountains, the fissures, the hills, and plateau. I could hear the men's labored, shallow breathing. One man's is quite wet. I do not yet miss the alphabet of trees, the birds, tall buildings, refined dress, tea time, and the luxurious meals of London. But I begin to miss Flo, her wise advice and unflagging aid. I want her by my side again. I listen and hear so many men dying out in the field.

My right hand is upon the bandage of one man and my left hand is tending the wound of the other when Sir Robert Napier and Richard Wellfield enter the tent.

"King Theodore has withdrawn into his fortress..." he be-

gins to say to Richard, then stops and stares at me. Sir Robert
Napier's tired face appears shocked and then generally disgusted, a silent explosion, when he sees what I am doing. Then
Sir Napier turns and leaves. I do not care about these wounded
men's country. I am a nurse.

Richard is exhausted, but well, and I rush to him.

"You are unhurt?"

He takes my hand and presses it into his own dirty, fin-
gerless one. "Yes, Ann, I am fine. Our army has suffered only
superficial wounds. We have killed over 500 Abyssinians, with
many more wounded." He looks about the tent. "Their men
were brave but our weapons were superior." He removes his
helmet and leans his rifle with my ribbon circling it in a far corner of the tent. "I must speak with Sir Napier. I shall return."
And he leaves, enters the impending darkness full of painful
incantations and names called out loud, the groans of the nearly dead and the stars that wink and shake their incredulous
silver smiles. The constellations know that they do not need us
any longer.

The remaining two patients are quiet. My dark hair is plastered to my scalp, clinging tenaciously. Ordinary moonlight
crawls about the tent, alighting upon a stiff chair, a table. I take
up a pen and paper and sit at the too small, makeshift table
and write.

*My Dearest,*

*In India I saw a half-naked sadhu whose lower half seemed
wrapped in a large turban of sorts and he was sitting upon a bed of
nails. When I asked him why he did such a thing, the translator told
me that he replied that his god had told him that he would remain*

unhurt as long as he believed and that, so far, it had been true. He grinned at me and stayed sitting upon his bed of nails. It was then that I realized that all is interpretation. For what about all our children lying about after a battle, did they too believe that they would remain unharmed?

And what about ghosts, unfurling from their bodies? I do not believe that Mrs. Tatterspol, the medium of Mrs. Thompson, could call them forth. For while we could find some comfort from the dead not completely disappearing from our lives, that is precisely what they do. Those that have died under my care are gone forever. It is science and fact and truth. Although they may live in our memories as Martin Farland has graciously done for me—for otherwise would he have not been forgotten?

I have come to Abyssinia to care for the soldiers, the men, and that is what I intend to do. I have longed to do so. My nursing skills have much improved and you shall be greatly impressed.

It has been several months since I have written to you. I realize now that I have been sorely remiss in our correspondence. I could use your advice in evaluating the treatment for the men, and your support. I do wish you were with me, here.

Yours

The wounded men are now quiet so I run to another tent and slip my letter into the hands of a boy who had accompanied our party. He has a yellow cloth wrapped about his head like a small turban, is barefoot, and is playing with a stick in the sandy soil. When I return to the tent Richard is sitting upon the writing table. His face is stricken; light from the stars begins to freckle his right jawbone. I can see the faint, white outline of his scar on his neck, a lumpy road. One of the men on the straw is whispering and his head is spasmodically jerking from side to side, his hand reaches upward, punctures the night above him. A candle is lit. There is the odour of dust and old clothes in the air. Richard Wellfield takes my hand, kisses it. All the heat has drained away from the day. I stumble toward him and his sad eyes seek out mine.

"It is difficult to maintain one's sanity during a time of war," he says. "There is too much injury all around."

I refuse to meet his eyes. "Yes, that is often the case, although some thrive upon dire circumstances."

"You know our side has few casualties. You shall not be allowed to harbor these enemy soldiers, much less work to improve their health. Sir Robert Napier cannot allow it." His damaged hand strokes the thin sheet of my hair. His mouth is down-turned. "I shall take care of them, Miss Russell." And he rises, relinquishing my hand, and walks toward his rifle.

I say, "I shall take care of them."

"No. That is neither a woman's job nor a nurse's job. It is a soldier's duty to dispose of the enemy."

"No, they are my patients, under my care, and I must help them in the manner I see fit."

"Please allow me, Miss Russell, for I do not want you to have nightmares." The rifle is rigid in his hand.

"Absolutely not. Please know this—they will not be the first patients to die under my care." But I did not say more, did not say "by my hand."

"I insist, for I cannot imagine you capable of such an act."

But I am already standing over the man whose head is moving to and fro and I grip his neck tightly with my hands. I squeeze. He fights me, with weakened hands he tries to pry my fingers but I hold on. He gasps. His eyes sweep across my face, back and forth as though he is reading sentences from a book. His back arches and his brown body flails. I must look at his face because I am standing closely above him and his features appear large and bloated although he is young, with dark eyes and hair, perhaps only nineteen. His lips become the blue of water. He is drowning and cannot call for help. His fingernails against my wrist, pawing, are turning the blue of sky. And he cannot reach any air. His legs begin to dance, to seize, moving to unheard music. We are too close to one another. It is an intimate moment. I hold on. His face locks upon mine. Richard Wellfield sets down his rifle and positions his remaining fingers over mine, squeezing both our hands harder and more firmly now. There is a last release from the man's throat as though a final bird had flown off, abandoning its branch. The patient's hands fall to his sides, his legs stop their dancing, and his head falls slightly to the side. Richard and I sigh and look at each other. The man's eyes are bulging from their sockets and his tongue snakes out from his mouth. It is a grimace I do not like to see, but I must.

I hurry to Richard's rifle and rush upon the other quiet patient whose eyes are closed. I steady the muzzle with my ribbon against his temple and pull the trigger. There is a loud noise and a sneeze of blood into the air on the other side of his head that drifts down like rain upon the floor. I briefly see his frozen, mindless face, eyes suddenly open and fixed upon nothing as if searching for the terrible noise. Richard does not move. I dislike the dead men's faces.

"There. It is all done," I say.

Richard Wellfield tries to hold me in his arms but I push him away. Perhaps he misunderstands me. He lifts his rifle from the ground where it fell, my ribbon still tightly bandaging it. He dusts it off, places it upon the table and sits in front of it. His face is contorted, contagious, as though peering at an accident upon some London street and unable to pass it by. His hair is heavy yet filigreed in the moonlight and candlelight. I want to peek below the current of his features, discover some serenity there, and swim in that. His eyes are etched by the darkness, and I cannot see their full narrative.

"You are going to be sent home tomorrow, Ann. Sir Robert Napier believes it is the best thing all around."

It is then that I search out Richard's shoulders and cry against them, big tears that run down and moisten his army shirt with wet claw markings. Wetness seeps out from my nose and my hair falls against my face. My crying reverberates against the tent and loudly comes back to me. There are small explosions in my mind. I am caught and there are consequences. It is the first time I feel ashamed. Candlelight asserts itself against my cheek. The dead men appear ravaged and yet sleeping. Both of them once young. I fasten myself to his shirt and he strokes my hair again, catching strands between the distance of his fingers. I feel terribly small and alone. After a time I push myself away and dry my eyes with the back of my hand.

"Thank you for all you have done for me, Richard Wellfield. I shall look forward to seeing you when you return to London, after you are done here. You have been a true friend and your attentions are much appreciated."

"Would you like me to stay with you here tonight, in only the most respectful manner, of course?"

"No, thank you, that will not be necessary."

"I will have the bodies removed immediately."

"Thank you, Richard."

And he hesitates before me as though he has more to say, but I turn away from him and he leaves. The bodies are dragged from their straw mattresses within a few minutes by two men wearing bloodstained white turbans crisscrossed upon their heads. The men are tall and thin and bend down quite low. I hear the bodies pulled a short distance and then abandoned with the mass of other bodies on the plateau. Most are dead and unmoving. A few moan into the earth or try to rearrange their injured limbs; however, in the dark they merely become a part of the landscape, far mountains or small hills or boulders jutting up suddenly from the ground. I stretch my arms into the night air and feel the breeze to be cooler, thin, and tired, much like me. I will not go out and help any more men. I will listen to them die. For the last time, I hold some Abyssinian soil in my fist and let it run through the fingers of my hand. From dust to dust.

I move the chair to the edge of my tent and sit. I watch two other nurses in their own faraway tents lit by candles talking to soldiers, no nursing duties to occupy them either. For all the wounded are from the other side. I blow out my candle and the partial moon, resembling Hera's delicate, white wings, circles about us. The ragtag stars multiply, thicken, pulse in the night sky, so full of life and a light that will disappear by morning. I do not want to see the ocean of dead men in the morning.

A soldier limps by, using his rifle as a walking stick, and then he stops before me. A turban beneath his British helmet is unwinding down his back. "Did you hear, Nurse? King Theodore has shot himself in the mouth at Magdala and his body was just discovered by the soldiers of the 33rd Regiment of Foot, near his gate."

I shake my head.

"He shot himself with a pistol Queen Victoria had given to him as a present at that. Now they are torching the city." And he limps on, mumbling, "We have won, Nurse, and have freed all the hostages unharmed." The comma of his back disappears into the darkness.

But I do not care about sides, for they are arbitrary. Most things are neither completely good nor completely evil.

I stand and survey the land beyond this plateau but cannot see the great fire burning in the distance. Perhaps it is too far away or behind a mountain. The queer thing is that I do feel more alive after the deaths of the two Abyssinian soldiers, oddly calmer, as is often the case when men ask to die. I survived their strange faces, yet my own mouth has grown sadder. I am weary yet cannot sleep. I watch my hand flutter in the moonlight, thinking that death, with its kiss of nothingness, its encompassing oblivion, the vanishing, is often easier than life. I understand the needs of my patients, their need for surrender, the astonishing black void, a need to drown and have their body swept away. I feel the motion of the stars above me. My hands blister beneath the moon's brutal and skinned light. I have been turned inside out like a cadaver in the dead-house. Richard Wellfield has witnessed it all. My first witness and helper. I have been discovered for who I really am and I am relieved and have been shamed. I have never lied to the dying. For I am dying also. Slowly. And there is no one about to help me.

I light the candle, move my chair to the table, and take up my pen and begin again.

*My Dearest,*

*I want to be with you as a nurse and assistant. I shall arrive in London soon and shall explain my circumstances to you. I am looking forward to my new life and to seeing you.*

*Most sincerely yours,*

Laurie Blauner is the author of five books of poetry and one other novel called *Somebody*. *Infinite Kindness* has received a 2005 Arts Special Projects award from 4Culture, an arts organization. Laurie Blauner has received an NEA, Seattle Arts Commission, King County Arts Commission, Artist Trust and Centrum grants and awards. Her poetry and fiction have appeared in *The Nation, The New Republic, Poetry, American Poetry Review, Field, The Seattle Review, Talking River Review* and many other magazines. Her web site is www.laurieblauner.com.